Praise for Joe R. Lansdale

"Hilarious. . . . Lansdale is a terrifically gifted story-teller with a sharp country boy wit."
—*The Washington Post Book World*

"Lansdale's prose, both laconic and sarcastic, is so thick with slang and regional accent that it's as tasty as a well-cured piece of beef jerky. Readers will want to savor each bite."
—*Milwaukee Journal Sentinel*

"Lansdale has an unsettling sensibility. Be thankful he crafts such wild tall tales."
—*Chicago Sun-Times*

"A storyteller in the great American tradition of Ambrose Bierce and Mark Twain."
—*The Boston Globe*

"Funny, compulsive . . . enjoyably raffish."
—*Esquire*

Books by Joe R. Lansdale

In the Hap and Leonard Series

Savage Season
Mucho Mojo
The Two-Bear Mambo
Bad Chili
Rumble Tumble
Captains Outrageous
Vanilla Ride

Other Novels

The Bottoms
Sunset and Sawdust
Lost Echoes
Leather Maiden

Joe R. Lansdale

Rumble Tumble

Joe R. Lansdale is the author of more than a dozen novels, including *The Bottoms*, *Sunset and Sawdust*, and *Leather Maiden*. He has received the British Fantasy Award, the American Mystery Award, the Edgar Award, the Grinzane Cavour Prize for Literature, and seven Bram Stoker Awards. He lives with his family in Nacogdoches, Texas.

www.joerlansdale.com

Rumble Tumble

A Hap and Leonard Novel

Joe R. Lansdale

Vintage Crime/Black Lizard
Vintage Books
A Division of Random House, Inc.
New York

FIRST VINTAGE CRIME/BLACK LIZARD EDITION, NOVEMBER 2009

Library of Congress Cataloging-in-Publication Data
Lansdale, Joe R., 1951–
Rumble tumble / by Joe R. Lansdale.
—1st Vintage Crime/Black Lizard ed.
p. cm.
ISBN 978-0-307-45551-2
1. Collins, Hap (Fictitious character)—Fiction. 2. Pine, Leonard
(Fictitious character)—Fiction. 3. Fathers and daughters—
Fiction. 4. Southwestern states—Fiction. 5. Automobile
travel—Fiction. 6. Middle-aged men—Fiction. I. Title.
PS3562.A557R8 2009
813'.54—dc22
2009027229

www.vintagebooks.com

Printed in the United States of America
10 9 8 7 6 5 4 3 2 1

For Jimmy Vines, with mucho respect.

Many of the towns and cities mentioned are real, but Hootie Hoot, Oklahoma, though inspired by a number of oddly named Texas and Oklahoma towns, does not exist. At least I don't think it exists. If it does, my apologies. The same goes for Echo, Texas. I've also made some minor changes in Texas and Mexican geography to suit my storytelling purposes.

J.R.L.

Heat not a furnace for your foe so hot
That it do singe yourself.
                    Shakespeare, *Henry VIII*

"Remember what Nietzsche said—'Live
dangerously.' "
"You know what happened to Nietzsche."
"What?"
"He's dead."
                    —Joan Crawford responds
           to Jack Palance in *Sudden Fear*

Rumble Tumble

1

An easy and convincing case could be made that my life has been short on successes, both financial and romantic, but no one could say with any conviction it has been uneventful.

In fact, of late, it had been so full of events, I concluded I had outlived my allotment of outlandish moments, and now the law of averages was on my side for pursuing a relatively tame existence. At least until old age set in and I took up residence in a cardboard box beneath the overpass on Highway 59, taking a dump behind a bush and licking secret sauce off old Big Mac wrappers for sustenance.

That was how I figured most of us baby boomers would finish the race. No Medicaid. No Medicare. No insurance. No couple of million stashed back for our dotage. Maybe not even the cardboard box. Hell, for that matter, we couldn't even be assured of a bush to shit behind.

My dotage was a ways off yet, but a lot nearer than I

liked to think. Though I had days when I wished I wouldn't make that geriatric goal—end up in a cardboard box, stiff and rotting beneath an overpass with one of those Big Mac wrappers clutched in my fist—nor did I wish to gain the better scenario of passing on to the great beyond via a crisp white bed in a nursing home with a plate of mashed green peas on my dinner tray and a tube in my dick.

My best friend, Leonard Pine, always says the best way to go is lying in bed listening to a Patsy Cline song, or watching the last fifteen minutes of Championship Wrestling, which was funny enough to kill you.

None for me, though. Times like that, when I was blue and thinking of my exit, I wished to go out between the legs of some wild redhead while striving for a double on a cool winter night, her hot breath in my ear, her fingernails buried in my ass like tacks in a bulletin board.

It could happen.

Currently, I knew the wild redhead. She was my age, forties, her life full of her own unique events. Including setting fire to the head of an ex-husband and beaning his brainpan with the business end of a shovel. But even though she might worry me some when near matches or farm implements, going out between her legs was, as I said, not such a bad way to pass, so I tried to stay within her proximity as much as possible these days, lest I feel a bit of a murmur, a flashing of life's events before my eyes. I could only hope if such a dire situation arose, she would be in the mood and I could fight off the inevitable for whatever time was necessary for me to selfishly satisfy myself.

But redheads have drawbacks. They can be trouble and they can mess up your law of averages, even when they don't mean to, even when they aren't directly responsible.

Trouble sticks to them like pork to a pig's ass, and if the trouble isn't on them, it's on someone close to them.

I know that sounds a little like astrology—the stuff about redheads, not pork—but then again, you been through what I been through, you might come to believe it. And even if I don't believe it in the long run, in the short run, well, I got to consider it.

For me all this got to rolling on a day when I was sorting my stuff in Leonard's barn, where it had been stored for the last few months.

Leonard had owned a house in town for some time now, and when a tornado took my place away, I moved into his old country place, and it wasn't so bad. Then he sold his house in town for pretty good money, had to move back to his country place, and now we were housemates.

Frankly, I felt put out. Even if it was his house. I went from sleeping in the bedroom to sleeping on the couch, and he made me clean up the place more than I liked.

We had roomed together before, for a short time, and it had been okay, but now I had gotten used to living alone again, and I was having a bad time of it. Worse yet, way things were going, I might be moving in with my nasty redhead any day. Brett had invited me, and I wanted to, but I was having so much trouble readjusting to Leonard, and I had known him for years, the idea of living with someone else was goddamn scary. I was suddenly concerned about skid marks in my underwear. Socks that didn't match. Farts, burps, and stink from the bathroom.

I wished my house hadn't blown away.

I wished I weren't so set in my ways.

I even wished I could find a good deal on a mobile home to move to the acreage where my house once stood. And if you knew how much I dislike mobile homes—those plyboard and aluminum tornado magnets in the pleasing shape of a shiny rectangle—you'd realize just how desperate I felt.

Then there was the other side of me. The one that always wanted a relationship. I didn't have a woman in my life, I was pouty and blue, and even watching the September lovebugs hump made me horny. Now I had met someone who had more to offer than just sex. Brains. Humor. A way with fire and shovels. Kind of a middle-aged man's dream, I suspect. And still, I hesitated.

Guess, when you come right down to it, you just can't make me happy.

Anyway, I was on my knees, sorting my stuff in Leonard's barn, which was essentially a gray, peeling, clapboard shell with a dirt floor. I had all my things in cardboard boxes, and I was trying to figure what I should keep and what I should get rid of. During the storm, a large part of my junk had been rained on, wind-blasted, and just generally screwed. Rats had been in it since, and some of the paper and cloth items had been chewed.

Over the last few months I'd been halfheartedly going through the stuff I'd gathered up after the storm. Going through it, not so much afraid of what I might find, but more afraid of what I might not find. Some part of my life gone.

The twister had knocked the largest part of my goods ass over tea kettle, blown them to hell, or maybe worse, all the way to New York City. Maybe up North some Yankee was looking at my books, wearing one of my shoes. Laughing at my photographs. My favorite pants might be in a tree somewhere. My record collection at the bottom of a lake. It was too goddamn depressing to contemplate.

I had just put a batch of ruined books in the trash box when Leonard came into the barn. He was wearing sweats and carrying two cups of coffee. He looked as if he was straight from the shower. His short kinky hair glistened and his face looked like buffed ebony. The sunlight shone brightly through the door behind him, and I could see steam rising up from the coffee, blending with the dust motes in the air. Leonard said, "You going to move in with her?"

I stood and brushed the dust off my hands. Leonard gave me a cup. "I don't know," I said, and sipped the coffee. It was good rich coffee with some kind of chocolate flavoring in it.

"You ought to."

"You trying to get rid of me?"

"Some. You're fuckin' up my house."

"Like it's anything special."

"Hey, it may be a shack, but it's better than your shack, which, I might point out, would be harder to put together than one of those thousand-piece landscape puzzles. If you had all the pieces."

"Touché."

"And the way you handle your domestic business, man, it's tiresome. Think I want to have your old smelly drawers hanging on my couch arms for doilies? Goddamn shoes in the middle of the floor, dirty old socks up under the chair. Hell, man, smells like someone's been wiping their ass and hidin' the paper somewhere."

"You're exaggerating."

"All right, then, your shoes are slightly off center of the middle of the floor. But I still trip over them. Now what about Brett? You movin' in with her, or not?"

"I've been burned so many times in love I'm not sure I want to go through it again."

"Yeah, but all your other relationships were stupid. This one isn't."

"She set her husband's head on fire, burned his car too."

"Don't forget she beaned him with a shovel and he's in a home somewhere trying to decide if blue socks go with a paper hat and a fart."

"There's that."

"Maybe she should have left the car alone, Hap, but way I see it, far as his head's concerned, sonofabitch had it comin'. Besides, she didn't burn his whole head up, just some of it. Guy beats a woman on a daily basis, and one day she's had enough, it's okay she sets the guy's head on fire."

"This coming from an arsonist."

"Don't bring that up. You're tryin' to change the subject. Law let me go, didn't they?"

"It was a miracle." And it was. Leonard had burned down three crack houses, and each time he'd managed to get off. 'Course, I helped burn down one of them, so I couldn't be too self-righteous.

"They let Brett go, didn't they?" Leonard said.

"The judge was a lecher. She was young then. She wore tight shorts and a halter top. I'm surprised they didn't throw her a parade and give her the key to the city. Way she looks now, back then, man, she must have been something."

"Being queer, it's hard for me to know what a good-lookin' woman's supposed to look like, but I figure Brett's it. She's got all her workin' parts, don't she?"

"Yeah."

"You get along, don't you?"

"Yeah. She's funny. I like being around her. We seem to have something going besides dating and rutting, although I hasten to add I don't want to undervalue rutting."

"Then what's the holdup?"

"I just don't want to screw up again."

"Hap, that's what you do best. And if you ain't willin' to screw up, you ain't ever gonna get any of the good out of life either. That's the way of the world, according to Leonard Pine. And keep in mind I just went through somethin' worse, and I'm out here lookin' for love all over again. It's the way of our species."

"We're a stupid species."

"Yeah, but we're consistently stupid. So, you get what I'm sayin'?"

"You're as big a screwup as me?"

"No one is, Hap. But thing is, even though you fuck up more than most, everyone fucks up. Only difference with you is you think your fuckups matter more than anyone else's. Strangely enough, there's a kind of conceit in all that."

"I reckon you're right."

"Good. Why don't you tell her you're moving in?"

"Because I'm still not sure."

"You see her today, right?"

"Right."

"She's expecting an answer, right?"

"Right."

"Do it."

2

I drank my coffee, sorted my junk awhile longer, put on my sweats, and Leonard and I went jogging along the road in front of his house and past my place, which now consisted of a bathtub. It was the only thing the tornado hadn't taken away. And good thing too. Brett had been hiding in it.

Sad as it was to pass the place by, I remembered the tub fondly. I had found Brett there after the storm. We had lain together inside the tub, and after the rain passed and the sky cleared, we held each other beneath the bright stars and the cantaloupe slice of quarter moon. Early in the morning, before full light, there in the cool damp tub, we had made love.

"You're dragging ass," Leonard said, jogging ahead of me.

"I'm getting fat," I said.

"I've noticed. Too many doughnuts. Too much late-night eating."

"It's a habit I've got. I eat when I think about Brett. I think about not being with her, I eat. I think about moving in with her, I eat."

"Frankly, Hap, ole buddy, I think you just eat."

"I hate it when you're right."

We jogged down the road a ways, then back again. It was a cool September morning, moving toward a warm afternoon, and the lovebugs were so thick in the air, you swatted at them, you brought down a whole squadron. They were present every year, but this was a bumper year, and according to old weather philosophy, the year they were the thickest meant the fall and winter would be extremely cold or rainy or both.

I was puffing pretty hard when we got back to Leonard's place. Leonard wanted to hang the heavy bag in the barn and work it some, but I decided it was time I bucked up and went over to see Brett, made a decision one way or another. She wasn't expecting me at an exact time, just before lunch, and it was now ten o'clock.

I showered, had another cup of coffee, went out to the barn and watched Leonard hammer the heavy bag for a while, then drove to Brett's in my junky Chevy Nova. I had owned the wreck about three months, and it was already due for the scrap yard. It clattered and coughed and blew black smoke out the rear like an old man with a gastric condition. I was ashamed to be seen in it, ashamed to pollute the air like that.

I had purchased the rolling calamity for three hundred dollars after my truck got destroyed during the tornado, and the way I saw it now, I'd paid about two hundred and ninety-nine dollars too much, even if it had come with a pack of rubbers in the glove box, half a cigar in the ash-tray, and air in three tires.

I had put air in the fourth tire, and one of these days I was going to toss out that cigar and the rubbers. There was also a row of hardened gum that had been mashed underneath the dash, and I had plans to remove that as well. So far the urge hadn't hit me. The most I had done to redecorate the Nova was put my .38 Smith & Wesson in the glove box on top of the pack of rubbers.

As I drove over to Brett's, I tried to decide what to say. What to do. Everything I thought of struck me wrong. Maybe we could just keep things like they were? Then again, I did that, eventually I'd lose her. I had to make up my mind one way or another, and suddenly I knew what the problem was.

I didn't feel worthy.

I worked a night job at a club, beating people up who misbehaved. What kind of job is that for a grown man? What did that offer a woman like Brett? I didn't even have a home, a decent car, or, for that matter, any decent clothes. I was just a goddamn vagabond living day to day on the grace and goodwill of friends like Leonard and Brett.

I had been raised by solid blue-collar folk, and they had reared me to respect and like myself, to have confidence, and for years I had plenty. But these past few years, it had begun to erode. I was a middle-aged man who still didn't have a career, and it looked less and less like I would ever have one.

What could I do? I was smart enough, but what were my credentials? Lifting big rocks? Eating dust in the rose fields? Slapping drunks upside the head, twisting their wrists, and throwing them into a parking lot? It wasn't much of a résumé.

And my looks weren't going to carry me through either. I was graying at the temples, balding at the crown, growing thick, and my face had a look of hound dog sadness about it, as if I had second sight and knew bad things were coming.

When I got over to Brett's she was sitting in an aluminum chair on the front lawn fighting lovebugs and mosquitoes. I could see her from the curb where I'd parked. I got out and went over there, smiling. Brett wasn't smiling, however, and I got a nasty feeling in my gut, like maybe I'd waited too long to make up my mind one way or another.

"You like bugs?" I asked.

"Not really," she said, and this time she smiled. It was a little strained, but it was a smile.

"You look like maybe you're smiling around something sour."

"I'm glad to see you," she said. "Especially now."

"Something wrong?"

"Yeah. Let's go inside."

Inside, we picked lovebugs out of each other's hair and opened the screen and threw them out. There was a pot of coffee on, and Brett poured us cups. We sat at the table, then she looked at me and tears began to squeeze out of her eyes and run down her cheeks.

"Brett, what's wrong, honey?"

"It's Tillie, Hap."

Tillie was Brett's wayward daughter. A young woman who had gotten mixed up in drugs and prostitution and whose last letter home was hopeful because her pimp had stopped beating her as much and her limp was better. Brett had tried to talk her out of the life, had offered to have us come get her, but she didn't want out, or didn't know how to get out, or it was some kind of stubborn pride thing. It was hard to say. Frankly, I tried not to involve myself unless Brett involved me.

"What's the score?" I asked.

"There's a man in a motel wants to talk to me about her. He called this morning. Says she's in trouble and I should talk to him."

"He didn't tell you what about over the phone?"

Brett shook her head. "He wants money."

"To tell you what kind of trouble she's in?"

"I'm supposed to go over there around one o'clock and bring five hundred dollars. I told him I had to have someone drive me. I didn't want to go there by myself."

"That's a smart idea."

"He said that was okay."

"I don't like the sound of it," I said.

"Neither do I, but he said Tillie was in deep shit and I ought to know about it. He said Tillie paid him some to tell me she was and that I'm supposed to pay him some before he tells me what the problem is, and he said if cops come he won't tell me anything and everything is off. But I come with one person and five hundred dollars, he'll tell me what I need to know."

"A real Good Samaritan."

"I got a gun," Brett said. "I can use it, and it's legal. But I still don't like going over there by myself, gun or not. Me with all that money. I don't know he's got someone with him or not. But him talking about Tillie like he knows her, I got to go see."

"No problem. We'll both go."

3

My wreck was iffy just driving into town, so we went in Brett's blue Plymouth Fury. Like me, she had recently traded cars, and though this one was many years old and not exactly a road racer, it had been regularly serviced, and could get up to seventy miles an hour without the assistance of a tow truck. It's also nice to be driven around town by a good-looking redhead, even if you're on a bicycle built for two.

On the way over to the motel the lovebugs pelleted the windshield and collected beneath the motionless wipers like dead soldiers in trenches, left greasy yellow and green spots all over the glass.

We got to the LaBorde Motor Inn about ten minutes before one and parked in front of a row of doors. I had brought the pistol from my glove box, and I stuck it under my shirt against my spine.

Brett has a thigh holster, and she wore a skirt so she

could wear the holster and the snub-nose .38 she owns. It's not that she goes around wearing a thigh holster and a .38, but recent events had led to this, and she has a license. In Texas, with the right training and certification you're allowed to carry a concealed handgun. It's a law Leonard loves and I hate, but I'm a hypocrite, because I keep a revolver in my glove box, and from time to time on my person. I'm even more of a hypocrite because, unlike Brett, I never bothered to get a license.

We walked to the metal stairs, went up and found the number the caller had given Brett, and knocked. Thirty seconds didn't pass before the door opened and a face showed over the chain inside the door, and it was some face. It looked like first base after a hot season in the Astrodome: pocked and beaten and not too clean. He stuck the face out enough so I could see his nose had been broken and some teeth with it, and recently. Behind the face I could see a body that looked as if it ought to be used to hold up something heavy. He took the chain off for a better look at us, and we got a better look at him. He wore a dirty white dress shirt and black pants with gray pinstripes and shiny black dress shoes, except for the toe tips, which looked to have been dipped in shit.

"You Brett?" he said.

Brett nodded.

"We told you not to bring nobody," he said.

"You, or whoever I spoke to, said I could have someone drive me," Brett said.

"We thought you meant some other woman," the face said.

"I didn't say that," Brett said. "What's it matter?"

"I don't know it matters," said the man, "but we didn't think you'd bring no man."

"Well," Brett said. "I don't know why you shouldn't have thought it."

"Hey," I said, "do I look dangerous to you?"

"Naw, you don't look dangerous," he said, and he walked away from the door and we followed inside.

The first thing I noticed was a midget sitting on the bed. I think that's normal, noticing a midget first. He had on a tailored blue Western suit and shiny blue cowboy boots and a gold cowboy shirt with silver snaps and a string tie with a silver cow head clasp holding it together. The suit looked as if it had once been expensive and nice, but now it was covered in filth and so was the shirt. The steer horns leaned a little too far left and somehow gave the midget an unbalanced look, as if he had been laid out without the use of a plumb line. I figured originally a hat had gone with the outfit, but now his blazing red hair was scattered over his head in such a way if you took a photo of it, it might look like a man with his head on fire, à la Brett's ex-husband. He had a big thick cigar in his mouth, but it wasn't lit, and his feet dangled off the side of the bed almost two feet from the ground. He had a face I couldn't judge for age. He might have been thirty or forty or fifty. For all I knew, he was twenty-one and constipated or had just previously passed a kidney stone.

Second thing I noticed was the big guy had drawn a little silver automatic out from behind his back. The rest of the room sort of lost interest for me after that.

The big guy sat down in a chair with his automatic and held it against his thigh. Next to his chair was a table lamp, and on the table was a glass containing a clear liquid that I guessed from the smell in the room wasn't water. And considering how rank our hosts smelled, this meant some goddamn serious drinking had been going on.

"What's the gun for?" I asked.

"He's the nervous type," said the midget.

"What about you?" I said. "You nervous?"

"No, I'm not nervous," said the midget. "Not as long as he's got the gun. Y'all sit somewhere."

Brett took a chair and I sat on the edge of the bed so I could see both guys. I said to the big guy, "You shoot that off, you got the noise to worry about."

"I'm not that worried," said the big guy.

"Drink?" said the midget.

Brett and I declined. Brett said, "One of you called me about my daughter."

"That was me," said the midget.

"Told me you had information and to bring money for it, and I have. Five hundred dollars."

"We should have said a thousand," said the midget.

"But you didn't," I said. "You said five hundred and here we are with it."

"It's all I got," Brett said.

"And we don't know what you got is worth five hundred dollars," I said.

The big guy said, "It might not be worth five cents, but we can take the five hundred dollars anyway."

I reached quickly behind my back, under my shirt, and pointed my gun at the big man. I said, "You might not."

The midget laughed. "You know, you could be right."

The big man wiggled the gun against his thigh like he wanted to lift it. I said, "Nope, nope, nope."

"Easy does it, Wilber," said the midget. "This man's got a look in his eye. Like someone who might have grown up on cowboy movies."

"Let's just have you put the gun on the table there, away from your drink," I said. "I wouldn't want to confuse what you might be reaching for."

The midget made with his odd laugh again.

Brett moved slowly and smoothly and her hand went under her skirt and came back out. She was holding the snub-nose. She pointed it at the midget.

"Oh, ho," said the midget.

"Just in case you got a gun too, shorty," Brett said.

"I got one," the dwarf said, "but it's in my suitcase."

"I told you that was a dumb place to put it," said the big man, placing his automatic on the table.

"Turns out you're right," said the midget. Then to me: "I thought you said a gun would make noise."

"It will," I said, "but like your buddy here, I'm not that worried about it. Now, you either got something to say, or you don't."

"We got plenty," said the midget. "First, I'd like to say you got good legs, lady."

"Thanks," Brett said. "My day's made."

"I'd also like to know what these bugs are all about. Is this a consistent thing here in East Texas?"

"Every year about this time," I said. "They're not usually this thick. Don't usually mate this long. Lots of them are supposed to signify a forthcoming bad winter or lots of rain. Might be both. Least that's the folklore."

"In Oklahoma we're having quite a run on mosquitoes," the midget said. "Big things. Very fat. They carry disease, you know?"

"We've got mosquito problems here too," I said. "And roaches. And June bugs. And all manner of squiggly-shit bugs who have names I don't know, but that's all the entomology lesson you get today. Tell us what you got to tell, or we walk. With the five hundred dollars."

"Walk, you don't learn about daughterpoo," said the midget.

"Yeah," I said, "but we walk after I pistol-whip the both of you, and what the two of you learn is it hurts."

17

"You look like a man would hit a midget," said the midget.

"You betcha," I said, and tried to sound convincing, the way Leonard would sound, because he was definitely a man would hit a midget, or anyone who fucked with him.

The midget touched his jacket, said, "I want to reach inside here, get a match and light my smoke. That okay?"

"No," Brett said. "I don't like it."

"I talk better I got a smoke," the midget said.

"I bet you can talk good either way," I said. Then to the big guy: "I'm liking where that gun is less and less. Brett, you mind taking it?"

Brett leaned over and grabbed the automatic off the table and dropped it onto her lap. She held the .38 on the big guy now. The big guy looked at the gun in her lap, then at her face, then at her gun. He grimaced, and considering how he already looked, it wasn't pretty.

I turned so I could lay my gun across my knee. That way it was easy to move and point at the midget should he find something inside his coat I didn't like, but it was a little less personal this way.

"I really would like to smoke," he said.

Brett nodded. The midget reached inside his coat and brought out a little folder of matches. He peeled one off and lit his cigar. The room turned foul quickly. He said, "This daughter you got, lady. She's in some manure up to her eyeballs."

"And you drove all the way down here to tell us," I said. "You're some good goddamn citizens, aren't you?"

"We drove down here 'cause we thought it might get us some money," the midget said. "And we need money. We're on our way to Mexico. Me and Wilber, we worked for Jim Clemente up until a day or so ago. But we had an unfortunate turn of events. We got our hand caught in the till, so to speak."

"Who's Jim Clemente?" I said.

"He's the main man in Tulsa, that's what he is. You want a whore, you buy one, somehow money goes back to him. Some little chippie in boogie town does a coon and gets ten bucks, Clemente, he gets six of it. You want someone killed, he's the one has it done. He has folks who do it."

"Like you two?" I said.

"Yeah, like us."

"What do you do?" Brett said to the midget. "Punch them in the butt?"

"It's not nice to make fun of a physical liability," said the midget.

"Look at it this way," Brett said, "you can drink out of the toilet without straining your back."

"That's no way to talk to a professional," said the midget.

"Professional, my ass," I said. "You didn't search either of us when we came in. You're about as organized as the Iraqi army."

"We been through some hard times," said the midget. "We're a bit scattered. And we aren't in that line of business anymore. By the way. They call me Red."

"I don't give a flyin' shit your name's God," Brett said. "You tell me about my daughter now, or I'm gonna shoot holes in your little kneecaps."

"My goodness," Red said. "What a foul-mouthed lady. I never could stand a woman cursed and talked tough."

"I'm not askin' you to stand it," Brett said. "I'm askin' you to stand bullet holes in your kneecaps. After that, maybe I'll shoot off the head of your little dick."

"Well," Red said, puffing his cigar. "I could ill afford that. Let me try and put it in a nutshell."

"You couldn't put it in a number ten washtub," Wilber said.

Red ignored him, said, "Wilber and I worked for Jim Clemente. We did odd jobs for him. We checked on things for him. One of the things we checked on was hookers. Your daughter, ma'am, is a hooker, and with the kind of mouth you have, I can see how she might have drifted from the straight and narrow. In my case, my old mama sold me to a carnival. I rode big dogs on a little red saddle. I had some acts with chimpanzees as well. Little rascals are always fornicating or defecating on something, and it doesn't bother them to throw dung either, I'll promise you that. Humiliating. It gave me a bad outlook on life. That and always looking at people's crotches."

Brett said, "I don't care you had to wear diapers, fuck a duck, and eat monkey shit."

"I just bet you don't, lady," Red said. He took hold of his cigar, turned it around in his mouth, pulled it out, blew smoke, put it back and looked at the toes of his boots. He said, "What I'm doing is trying to find a place to begin."

"Just about anywhere is starting to look good," I said.

"Then, I suppose I should start with the strangulation of Maude Fields. Does that seem appropriate to you, Wilber?"

"That'll work," Wilber said.

4

The air-conditioning unit cut off and back on. A blast of cold air filled the room. Red said, "This Maude was a madam out of Oklahoma City. She worked for Jim Clemente. Not that she wanted to, but if Jim decided you were working for him, then you were working for him. Like I said, some whore put out for money somewhere, Big Jim, he knew about it and you owed him. Someone snorted some coke or sold a rock, he got a share. He was fair in his own way. Maude got the largest cut of the meat she was selling, but Jim, he got a share, and it got so Maude was obstreperous. Holding out. She'd been warned. More than once. Jim can be a very warm and understanding guy, but he doesn't like to warn someone more than twice.

"He sent me and Wilber over to Oklahoma City to have a talk with her. She was most inconsiderate. Not unlike the lady there with the revolver. Very rude. Very . . . how

21

shall I put it. Very . . . Go Ahead. Well, our orders were simple. Either she came through, or we eliminated her and set something up new for Jim. She didn't come through. In fact, she tried to shoot the both of us with a derringer. That didn't work out. She missed. Wilber disarmed her and held her down and I strangled her with a stretch of piano wire strung between two wooden knobs. It sounds exotic. Almost secret-agent-like. But it's really a messy instrument. They say a gun is messy, but I must tell you on authority this isn't true. I suppose a bullet makes a kind of mess, but it's from afar if you want, and if you get a good shot in, and you don't shoot your target in your living room, you just walk off.

"Not so strangling a colored woman who I would judge tapped out at about three-fifty and could tie a good-sized hog in a knot with her bare hands. Wilber had to sit on her, and I had to hold her head in my lap and use the piano wire on her throat. Very messy. Gets all over you."

"Yeah, and she shit herself," Wilber said.

"Yes," said Red, "there was that. Defecation. Most unpleasant. I was reminded of the chimpanzees I used to work with."

"Had on a muumuu," Wilber said. "It ran down her legs. Got on my hands, all over my pants and shoes. Had to throw them away. The pants, not the shoes. Shoes cleaned up all right."

"It took us a good part of a half hour to finish her," Red said, "and I bet that piano wire cut all the way to the bone, and still she struggled. I've never seen anything like it. The woman was a regular Rasputin."

"And she just shit all over everything," Wilber said.

"You said that," I said.

"Seemed the more I tightened that wire, the more she fought," Red said. "Wilber there, big as he is, couldn't hold her down. When it was over, we were both exhausted. It was quite a rumble tumble."

Red looked at Brett to see what effect he was having. Brett's face held no more emotion than the revolver in her hand. I could see a flash of disappointment roll over Red's face, but he covered it with a puff of his cigar. A cloud of dark tobacco smoke rolled up and gathered about his red head like smoke above a forest fire. Red leaned over and thumped his ashes in an ashtray on the nightstand next to the bed.

"You telling this so we'll know how tough you are, or just because you like to hear yourself tell it?" I said.

"Both," Red said. "And Maude has to do with Tillie, and that has to do with Jim, and finally with us, then you. I'm wanting you to know too, that though Wilber and I have had our disagreements with Jim, I think Jim is one heck of a good fella."

"Ain't no one nicer to niggers," Wilber said. "He's got lots of niggers work for him, and Indians, and that's more than can be said for folks down this way."

"Jim is quite advanced when it comes to equal opportunity employment," Red said.

"He's got some old niggers work for him too," Wilber said. "He'll hire an old nigger fast as a young nigger. 'Course, just for certain jobs."

"Frankly," I said, "Jim's work relations don't interest us all that much."

Red nodded. We were all close friends now. "Big Jim does have his problems, however. Gambles too much."

"He'll gamble on anything," Wilber said. "I've seen him bet on how long a guy's dick would be. And that fella had to get it out too, and Big Jim, he could guess a thing like that."

"But he isn't homosexual, or anything like that," Red

said. "He just likes to gamble, and the wilder the gamble, the more he likes it. Always pays up when he loses too. 'Course, he don't lose much. Big Jim's a character. All in all, you couldn't ask for a nicer more honest employer in this type of business."

"Tell us about Tillie," Brett said.

"Well, Tillie worked for Maude. She was one of Maude's girls, you see. When we did Maude in, we put the old reprobate in a piano crate with about three hundred pounds of rocks to keep her company, drove her all the way to Arkansas and dropped her hefty self in a lake. We made it a kind of holiday, stopping to see scenic markers and points of interest along the way, though we drove over there faster than we drove back. She started to acquire an aroma about the time we got to the Arkansas line. When we completed the chore, we returned to Tulsa to see Jim. Jim was so pleased, he put me in charge of Oklahoma City and sent Wilber with me as a kind of enforcer.

"Let me say that the two of us merchandised more tail than Maude had sold in her lifetime. She had been holding out on Jim, but she hadn't been doing anywhere the business she could have. We set up little safaris, had girls hauled across state lines, doubled our truck stop business, and set up new houses in Texas, Louisiana, and Arkansas. We even had a traveling trailer we drove about Oklahoma, hitting the high spots. You wouldn't believe how easy it is to slip a girl into a rest home to help some old codger enjoy his last days. They'll blow six months' snack allotment for one good night with a woman. Some who hadn't had an erection in years were astonished to discover they could manage quite nicely with the right stimuli.

"I'm sure our girls hastened a few deaths that way, but

considering the alternatives, I doubt the old fellas really minded. Besides, when you're seventy-five or so, after a full-course dinner and a slice of young tail, what else you got to look forward to?

" 'Course, you got to bribe lots of interns and nurses and stuff, so it's not quite as profitable as it should be."

"About Tillie," Brett said.

Red nodded. "The traveling trailer was, in many ways, our busiest little sideline. Your daughter was part of that recreational tour from time to time, Ms. Brett."

"Then you were Till's pimp these last few years?" Brett said.

"I suppose you could say that," Red said, "though it doesn't have quite the professional ring I prefer. I like to think of myself simply as a businessman, and Wilber here as the pimp."

"Yeah," Wilber said. "I'm the pimp. I keep the girls in line. I take care of the johns don't want to pay, and if shit goes on some place I ain't, we got . . . had . . . fellas took care of things for us."

"We were doing quite well selling women," Red said. "So we were able to give Jim almost double what Maude had been giving him, and still there was money, and, well, I hate to admit it, but greed got the better of us. We thought since Jim was making double what he was making before, he'd be happy, and not realize we were making almost as much as he was."

"But he found out," I said.

"I'm afraid so," Red said.

"Man," said Wilber, "we fucked up a sweet business."

"Yes, we did," Red said. "It became necessary that we depart. Some of Jim's men paid us a visit, and but for the grace of the devil they would have killed us, but Wilber here fought dynamically, disposing of a couple of the hoodlums with his bare hands. I shot two of them to death, but not before I was roughed about quite a bit. My suit shows the activity. And you can see the damage to Wilber's face. A rumble tumble on the same par as that with the colored woman. Perhaps brisker.

"Preparing to depart, we discovered we were financially embarrassed. We made a lot of money, but we spent a lot of money. This suit alone, designed to my specifications, cost six hundred dollars. Can you imagine that? There's not enough actual material here for a good-sized throw rug. But, we had no money, so we had to ask the girls for money."

"You asked?" Brett said.

"Well, we actually persuaded them it was good idea. Guess what? They had very little. Considering Jim and ourselves took a nice chunk of their earnings, and allowed them to spend the bulk of the remainder through us for supplies, well, whores are not very rich. Your daughter, however, had managed to save some money and she offered it to us without any persuasion. It was only five hundred dollars, but with the rest we had from the other girls we acquired just short of a thousand. Not a lot for men who normally spent that in a day, but beggars couldn't be choosers.

"Your daughter gave us the money and said if we would come here and tell you that she wants out, and that she needs help to get out, you would give me another five hundred dollars."

"You did this for five hundred dollars?" I asked.

"McDonald's pays considerably less a week for tossing burgers, sir," Red said, "and at the moment, every little drop helps. If we can scam out on this motel bill before they realize our credit cards belong to a colored man we mugged in Amarillo out back of a barbecue joint, we can start rolling promptly, steal a car closer to the Mexican border. We might just manage to elude anyone Jim sends after us. Once in Mexico, five hundred dollars becomes two or three thousand, you use it right. Then we can have some breathing room. Perhaps run some whores down there. There's always some sort of enterprise going on in Mexico, though much of it seems to involve the use of knives and guns."

"You ought to be used to that," I said.

"The degree of excitement is higher down there," Red said. "I've lived there before. Shortly after I departed the circus. Unlike Americans, Mexicans—though short-tempered and fond of sharp weapons—seem to appreciate a midget."

"Where is Tillie?" Brett said.

"I've written the location down," Red said. "May I reach in my pocket?"

"Carefully," I said.

Red brought out a piece of paper and handed it to me. I took it and opened it and looked at it. "You could just be picking up five hundred dollars," I said. "This could be a Laundromat."

"Could be," Red said. "But it isn't."

"It isn't even Oklahoma City. What the hell is Hootie Hoot?"

"I know how it sounds," Red said. "But it's a real town. It's a little burg outside of Oklahoma City. We actually found it to be quite a refuge, and it provides easy access to the city, and frankly, most men who wanted to purchase sex didn't want to pay for it in a place they thought there might be law. This burg, cops were paid off. They liked a little regular tail themselves, see. We get the five hundred dollars or what?"

I looked at Brett. Brett stood up and tossed me Wilber's

gun. I caught it and dropped it on the bed between my legs. Brett lifted her dress and took five hundred dollars out of the end of the thigh holster. We all checked out the thigh holster and what it was strapped to. In the light I could see little freckles on Brett's thigh, like the blush on a strawberry.

Brett put the revolver in the holster. The five hundred was folded. She unfolded it. She stood next to the table lamp where Wilber sat and counted it out aloud, dropping each bill on the table.

"How does it look?" Red asked Wilber.

Wilber picked up the money and thumbed through it. "Like five hundred dollars."

"Good," Red said. "Good."

Wilber sniffed the money. "And it smells like a woman's thigh."

"Even better," Red said.

"You said Till was in trouble," Brett said. "Besides being a whore in Big Jim's stable, how's she in trouble?"

"It's my guess the other girls will tell that she helped us willingly, to help herself get out. Big Jim doesn't like that sort of thing. He'll have a special work plan for her."

"What's that mean?" I asked.

"It means she won't like it," Red said. "As for what he'll have in mind for her, I can't say. Maybe he'll put her on the street in Tulsa. Some other place not even that nice."

"Then this address could be meaningless?" I said. "Probably is by now."

"It's the last address where she was," Wilber said.

"Correct," Red said. "That's all we know."

"That's not worth five hundred dollars," I said. "That's worth a sack of dog shit."

Red looked at Brett. "Ma'am."

"Keep the money," Brett said.

"All right," I said. "This is where our association ends. I don't want to ever see either one of you again. I do, I might not like it."

"Suits me," Red said. "I haven't found either of you particularly sociable."

"I ain't scared I see you again," Wilber said. "I think you ain't near tough as you think you are."

"You're the one with the broken nose and the fucked-up teeth," I said.

Red laughed.

"Yeah," Wilber said, "but wasn't you did it."

"That's true," I said, and moved quickly and shot my foot out and hit Wilber in the mouth. His head went back and hit the wall and he came out of the chair charging. I sidestepped and brought my gun down behind his ear. He fell down and I kicked him again. A tooth slid under the bed and I could see a piece of another in my tennis shoe with a bloody spot around it.

It wasn't really necessary, but I bent over and hit Wilber one more time behind the ear with the revolver. "That's because we heard Till's pimp beat her. And if you weren't the one, my best apologies."

Wilber moaned, rolled over on his back. "Bastard," he said. "I might want to see you again sometime."

"Your choice," I said. "But I don't recommend it."

Red recovered his matches and was relighting his cigar, which had gone out. The only thing he had done during the action was raise his feet a little. He said, "Now you got the news on Tillie, might I suggest you forget it. Taking one of Jim's whores is not a good idea. He frowns on all manner of business tampering, and we are living proof of that, and the fact that we're living proof is rare. The whores, they do what they're told, and they stay where they're told, and they don't want to do that . . . Well, they still do it."

"I'd like to see you tangle with Big Jim," Wilber said from his position on the floor. "I'd like you to tangle with me when I'm ready."

I didn't say anything to that.

Brett opened the door. I took hold of Wilber's automatic and popped out the clip. I wiped the automatic with my shirt, threw it on the floor. I put the clip in my shirt pocket. I held my gun next to my leg and Brett and I walked out of there and closed the door and went along the walk quickly, down the stairs, out to her car.

I took Wilber's ammunition clip out of my pocket, wiped it with my shirttail, and dropped it into the parking lot.

When Brett was behind the wheel and I was beside her, she looked at me, said, "Surreal."

"Yeah," I said. "What now?"

"A light lunch. Sex."

"With me?"

"Unless you can suggest someone else."

I shook my head. "Nope. Don't think so. Nobody comes to mind, anyway. We could check the want ads, you like."

"Nah, you'll do."

5

On the way to Brett's house, I felt her mood go dark. She had suddenly realized just what kind of people her daughter was involved with. It's not that she hadn't known before, or hadn't tried to convince Tillie to give it up, but now, with Tillie wanting out, and her seeing scum like Red and Wilber, she knew the world of her daughter firsthand. It's one thing to wave at the devil from afar, quite another to shake the bastard's hand.

Brett didn't say a word about how she felt, but I could feel the change in her, tangible as the taste of a stinkbug in your last spoonful of custard.

And speaking of which, the lovebugs were worse. They came at the car like bullets, splattered and spurted their grease across the windshield until it was impossible to see. Brett had to pull over at a serve-yourself filling station. I got out and pumped gas and tried to clean the windshield with the water hose and a paper towel, but it wasn't a very good job. The water just mixed with the bug goo and spread itself over the windshield like film over a dying eye.

Back in the car, I said, "How about that light lunch?"

"Sure," Brett said, then she began to cry. I slid over and put my arm around her and kissed her cheek, which was wet with tears. She said, "I know now she's in trouble. Hell, I've known that all along. Why didn't I do something?"

"You tried to talk her out of it."

"I should have gone up there and got her."

"She wouldn't have come."

"She wants out now."

"That's now," I said.

"She could be dead."

"No reason to think that. Guy like this Big Jim, he doesn't kill his stock over something like that. Meat on the hoof is how he sees it. It'll probably be like Red said. A punishment of some kind. Hooking where she wouldn't want to hook."

"I can understand fucking," Brett said, "but for money, and with anybody, and with someone telling you what to do. And all kinds of disease. Some of the men . . ."

"I know."

"I can't believe I'm boo-hooing like this. It's embarrassing."

"Shouldn't be."

"But it is."

"Hell, I cry, Brett."

"Does it mess up your eye makeup?"

"Absolutely."

She smiled, said, "I could call the cops, and maybe do something there, but a hooker, I don't think they're going to be all that concerned. They were, this Big Jim wouldn't be doing business like he's doing."

"Some cops are concerned," I said. "Most. It's just not that simple. Guys like Big Jim know how to do bad business and have people know it's bad business, and still get away with it."

"Then I've got to go get her. Hap, I have to."

"I know."

The light lunch was at Brett's place, a tunafish sandwich with sweet apple slices in it, ice tea with lots of ice and no sugar, potato chips, and sweet pickles forked from a jar. We sat at the kitchen table and ate slowly and talked awhile, tried to figure what to do.

I said, "You know this isn't going to be a walk in the park?"

"Yes. I know."

"We're not going to drive up there and say 'We've come to get Tillie. Sleepover is finished.' It's not that easy."

"I know."

"It could turn ugly."

"I understand that. I'm not askin' you . . ."

"You are and you aren't," I said. "We've been over that. I'm not saying I won't go. I've already said I would. All I'm doing is warning you. We go up there, it could still turn out bad for Tillie."

"You think, as is, it's going to get better?"

"No, I don't. I guess I'm actually telling you what you can expect for yourself. It might be best you stay here, let me go."

"I wouldn't let you go by yourself."

"Leonard and I would go."

"You don't know he'll go."

"Yes, I do. But if he didn't, couldn't, I'd still go. And this is more something me and him can handle."

"You're sure?"

"No. But it sounds good."

Brett turned her glass of ice tea around and around in her hand, said, "I can't let you go by yourself. You go, with or without Leonard, I go too."

"What about your job?" I asked.

"What about yours?"

"I can leave it. It's not like I wasn't looking for a job when I found that one."

"I can get off too."

"You're sure?"

"I'm sure. It might make my supervisor's butt hole suck wind, but I've got some more vacation time coming. I need to get off, I can."

"All right," I said. "But you got to consider some things. These guys, they probably knew Tillie, all right. They may have worked for this Big Jim, but we don't know they're telling the exact truth."

"I guess I have some doubts, them driving all the way down here for five hundred dollars."

"Actually, I buy that," I said. "Scum like that, they'll do anything for a buck. They've probably robbed and looted every damn thing they could on their way down here. They figured since they were en route to Mexico, they might as well stop by and pick up five hundred bucks from you. We don't even know for sure Tillie wants you to come get her, or that she told them to ask for five hundred dollars. They may just know you're her mother, and nothing else. This could all be some story they made up. A grain of truth here and there, like a couple of whole corn kernels that have passed through the bowels on their way to becoming shit."

"That's metaphorical talk for you think they could be lying a lot. Right?"

"Right."

Somehow we drifted toward the bedroom, and it was very cool in there, and the sheets were soft and sweet-smelling and Brett was warm and even sweeter, and I kissed her lips, then her breasts, pausing to roll my tongue around and over her hard nipples. I ran my tongue down the length of her long legs, and kissed where she had shaved herself, then I kissed everything else there was to kiss, rolled her on her stomach, moved her legs apart, and entered her.

Brett had the CD going, playing *The Best of Percy Sledge*—which means anything he ever sang. The song was "When a Man Loves a Woman," and the way he sang made time stop. We made love for a long time, and eventually I had no idea which song was playing, and finally, when we finished, both of us satiated, I was somehow startled to realize we lay hugging each other in silence.

After a while, Brett said, "Now, that was some fuck."

"Yeah," I said, "and next time, I'm going to put my whole thing in."

"Yeah, right," Brett said. "What I meant to say, was that was some fuck, considering what you have to work with, and I don't mean me, pardner."

"Oh ho."

"Ho ho."

"Ho, ho, ho."

"Oh, ho, ho, ho."

We lay there for a while, kissing. Brett said, "You know, what we been talking about. About you and me."

"Me moving in?"

35

"Yeah. I still want that. But right now, I don't know we should. I don't know how things are—"

"I understand."

"—and Tillie, we go get her, well, I may need to keep her here, and with you and me trying to work things out together right now, I don't know."

"I understand."

"Well, don't understand too goddamn quick, mister. I want to do it, but maybe right now isn't good. It could put a strain on all of us that we don't need at the moment."

"It'll be all right."

"I love you, Hap."

"And I love you."

"It's okay we wait?"

"Sure."

"Want to stroke the bald beaver again?"

"Will it bite?"

"Absolutely."

We made love again. Less passionate this time, but satisfying nonetheless, then we lay with pillows propped behind our heads and Brett got the remote off the nightstand and turned the television on.

We lay there and watched some stupid talk show with a pig that was supposed to play a harmonica. The pig seemed bored. His owner held the harmonica, and the pig, a red neckerchief tied around its throat, tried to be cooperative and made a halfhearted attempt to blow into it. He could make a noise, but I wouldn't call it music. The pig's owner claimed it was taps.

Frankly, unless the sonofabitch can hit more than one note, I'm not that impressed with harmonica-playing pigs. In fact, way I feel these days, I don't know one could actually play taps, or even "The Star Spangled Banner," would excite me much.

36

We lay there holding each other, watching this pig, and finally some other program even more bland, then nothing. We fell asleep in each other's arms, the TV going, and when we awoke in the late afternoon a famous talk show host was trying to help some whitebread woman in a five-hundred-dollar dress sell a book she'd written on the power of love; about how all we had to do to make things right was just believe in love and it would fill the air.

Pollution fills the air, honey, you believe in it or not. Love takes more work than that. And unlike pollution, sometimes love goes away.

6

When I got back to Leonard's place my car windshield was caked with bugs. I used the hose and an old rag to clean it, but it wasn't a much better job than I had done on Brett's car at the filling station. Just call me Greasy Bill.

After I had been struggling for a while, Leonard came out of the house with a squeegee and gave it to me. I assumed he had been watching me through the window and had become frustrated. I used the squeegee and the hose and finally got the windshield clean. All the while I was doing this, I was glancing at Leonard out of the corner of my eye. I could see he was in a foul mood. He had that pouty mouth with the wrinkled forehead he gets when he's ready to jump your ass. Not the look where his eyes are on fire and you know someone is going to get mauled or maybe die, but the one tells you he's pissed and ready to let you know.

I tried some polite conversation about the bugs and the

weather. Pointed at a couple of interesting birds I saw on fence posts, but Leonard wasn't having any of that. I tried a clever slide into talking about Brett and her daughter, but he wasn't having any of that either.

He said, "Before we talk any outside shit, we're gonna talk some inside shit. I mean mine and your shit. Come on."

I followed him into the house. He said, "Sit down right there and wait a minute."

I sat on the couch. He left the room. A moment later he returned. He was carrying a roll of toilet paper and a toilet paper roller. "I'm gonna show you a little trick, here, Hap. You see, when you use the last piece of shit paper on your nasty ass, you take the roller post, that's this thing here, long and hard, unlike your dick, I'm sure. And you take this long and hard thing, the dick we'll call it, so it'll be something you can understand, and we take this dick, and we put it in the hole in the toilet paper tube.

"And in keeping with your mental faculties, we will call this hole in the toilet paper tube the pussy. So you take the dick, put it in the pussy, then, finished, you realize that the dick is sticking in the pussy and out the asshole, which is what we'll call the other side of the tube. You take each end of the dick, 'cause somehow it got broken off, okay, and you take each end of the dick and slip it into the little notches that hold it on to the wall in the bathroom. This way, you got a new roll of crap paper on a stick. That simple enough for you, Hap?"

"Good grief, Leonard. Don't have a cow."

"Yeah. Well there ain't nothing like taking a big ole greasy crap and having to duck-walk over to the cabinet to get another roll while you got a goddamn hunk of turd hanging out of your ass. You ought to try it some time."

"Not my sport."

"Let me ask you something, Hap. Who you think's been puttin' the paper on the goddamn roller?"

"Elves?"

"No. Let me ask you something else, Hap. Can you now, after instruction, put the dick in the pussy?"

"What if the paper tube has a headache?"

"Don't push me, Hap. I'm not finished here. Pay attention."

Leonard put the roller and paper on his easy chair. He opened the closet door and pulled out a broom. He got down on his knees by the couch, said, "Lift your feet."

I did. He swiped the broom under there and came out with a pair of formerly white, now gray, jockey shorts, festooned in cobwebs, bearing a couple of dead roaches like stickpins.

"These ain't mine," Leonard said. "These here are your ole nasty drawers. You've had them under there since you first moved in here. I go to clean today, and what do I see?"

"The toilet paper elves?"

"Your shitty drawers."

"My guess is, same elves been putting that paper on the roller have been fucking around with my underwear."

He stuck the broom and underwear in my face. "Got a shit stain in the seat. Your trademark."

"Careful, you could put an eye out with them drawers."

"These are yours, Hap."

"How the hell would you know? You check out my shorts every night? Could be one of your old boyfriend's."

"They ain't no old boyfriend's, 'cause I don't mess with men don't wipe their ass good, and they ain't mine, 'cause I don't take off my drawers in the living room and kick'm under the couch. That's a Hap Collins trademark. That and pissin' around the toilet, not just in it. You go in that bathroom, stand by the crapper, that goddamn rotten-ass piss on the floor will suck your shoes off and dissolve them."

"Well, you ought to clean more often, that way there wouldn't be underwear under the couch, or pee-pee on the bathroom floor."

"Hap, you're askin' for it, man."

"Way I see it, those elves can put a roll of paper on a stick, they ought to be able to get underwear out from under couches and wipe around the base of the commode, and you and I could just hang easy."

"You are *asking* for it, man. Let me question you somethin' else: when's the last time you cleaned anything in this house? We're gonna have to have a come-to-Jesus meetin' on that, my friend. And you ate the last vanilla cookie. Those are mine, Hap. Mine."

"I apologize. We were all out of steak. And if you think you're blue now, I'm going to throw more color on you. Me and Brett, we're not moving in together."

Leonard lowered the underwear onto the floor and tossed the broom down. "Ah, hell. Y'all have a fight?"

"No."

Leonard picked up the roller and paper and sat down in the chair and held them in his lap while I explained.

When I was finished, he put the roller and paper on the floor and walked over to the shabby fireplace and plucked one of his pipes from the pipe rack on the mantel, grabbed his bag of tobacco, unrolled it, and filled his pipe. He picked up a box of matches, returned to his chair, and studied me a moment.

"What you're sayin'," he said, kicking back in his easy chair and sticking the pipe into the corner of his mouth, "is, in a nutshell, this gal, this Tillie, decides to be a whore, then times get hard and she's ready to quit and they won't let her quit?"

41

"That's it."

"She think whoring had a retirement plan?"

"I don't think she thought at all."

"I don't even know this girl, Hap. There's lots of whores out there. Why, if I decided to save one, would I pick this one?"

"Because she's Brett's daughter."

"I don't know Brett that well. I mean, I like her, but I don't know her that well. You know this isn't going to be an easy thing. Just drive up there and knock on the door and help this whore carry her suitcase out to the car."

"Exactly what I told Brett."

"You're going, I go or not, aren't you?"

"You bet. So's Brett. She insisted."

"This Brett, she's got you by the ying-yang."

"The ying-yang. The balls. The heart. She's got me, man. And she's not asking me to do this. I'm volunteering."

"Oh, she's asking all right. I know you, a good-lookin' woman comes along and plays the right tune, you dance."

"All right, let's say she's asking. I love her. Why shouldn't she ask? Who else is she going to ask? I've done more for people I didn't care about as much, so why shouldn't I do it?"

"Because you might get your ass shot off. And considering you got one of them little narrow white asses, you can't spare much."

"You got enough for both of us."

Leonard let that one go by. He pulled a match, lit his pipe and puffed. "I reckon we get this over with, and Brett has time to settle stuff with her daughter, then maybe she'll take you in."

"That's the plan."

"We get this done, then maybe a short time after, I can get rid of you."

"That's possible."

Leonard nodded. "What we're going to need first is a few guns. I think for something like this, we're gonna need a few unmarked guns. I got a shotgun fills that bill, but we could use some other stuff."

"You're always with the guns."

"What do they shoot at us with when we do stuff like this, straws full of spit wads?"

"No."

"What then?"

"All right, I'll say it. Guns. Happy?"

"Yep. Now, we're gonna need guns. Correctomondo?"

"I suppose."

"I know you don't like the gun talk, Hap, but you know well as I do, at some point those people up there, they're who I think they are, they're gonna point guns at us. And the guns are gonna be loaded, and when they pull the trigger our heads are gonna go away. Unless we shoot first or intimidate their asses into not shooting at all. Maybe that way, we don't have to shoot. We throw the whore in the car, then drive like bastards."

"It's not my plan to go up there with guns blazing. I don't work like that."

"I know. I just said as much. We take it easy if the easy way is there. But it isn't, we got to go the hard way, then we got to be prepared. There's this guy I know, he can help us."

I thought awhile. Anytime talk of guns comes up, I get nervous. I don't like them. I was about the best goddamn shot with a rifle or handgun you ever saw, but I still didn't like them. I own one, and I still don't like them. I knew there were times when they were necessary, and it was better to have one and not need it than to not have one and need it, but goddammit, I still don't like them.

I sighed. "This guy you know. When can we see him?"

"I've mentioned him before. Haskel. You don't call him. You don't plan. You just go over to his place and be real careful."

7

This guy Leonard knew sold cold guns was named Haskel Ward. He lived down in the river bottoms about fifty miles from where we lived, not far from the Louisiana border. I had never been to Haskel's, but I knew where he lived and a little about him from hearing Leonard talk. Not that he had a lot to say about Haskel, but the name had come up, and what little he did say about him was not endearing.

Next morning, on our way to Haskel's, we drove through town in Leonard's new Dodge Ram, which was a treat he had given himself when he sold his house. We stopped at a fast-food place and had one of those breakfasts that has so much cholesterol in it the damn thing comes with a vein pump. After breakfast, I found a pay phone and called Brett.

"I'm off work for a couple of weeks, Hap," she said.

"That way, we go get Till, I can have some time with her before I go back to work."

"That's good."

"I'm packing a few things now."

"That's good too. Keep it light. But we're not going today."

"We're not?"

"Leonard and I have to pick up a few things."

"What kind of things?"

"Just be patient. I know you want to go right away, but we go, we got to be prepared."

"In what way? Packing a lunch?"

"Guns. Cold guns."

"Cold?"

"They aren't registered. They can't be easily traced."

"Oh. When are we going then?"

"My guess is we get the guns today, take care of some last-minute business the next day, then we go."

"Then maybe I should work tomorrow."

"If you can, you should. Don't plan on leaving until day after tomorrow. It's best when you do something like this you don't run off with your fly down and your dick hanging out. Or in your case, a tit."

"Not out of my fly though. I'm not that droopy yet."

"Darling, you aren't droopy at all."

"And most of the time you aren't either."

"I'll call you tonight."

By midday it was humid as a monkey's armpit down in the bottoms where the trees grew close together and right up next to the road. The moss and vines hung from the trees like alien spiderwebs and the birds were thick and colorful and loud and fluttered about like living Christmas ornaments.

46

We rode down the red-clay road with the air-conditioner on and the windows rolled tight, and the lovebugs, dense as back home, swarmed the truck from all sides and splattered against it like kamikazes.

Eventually the little red road played out at a dead end where a clapboard house three shades below gray stood amongst tall grass, a broken tricycle, an ancient Ford truck on blocks, an old wrecker with an oily winch. There were three young kids in the yard, two boys and a girl who looked as if they might bathe if they were pushed into a creek at gunpoint, held under with a foot, and beat with soap.

There was a chinaberry tree off to the right, and we parked under that next to a rusted outboard motor and a very old carcass that may have once been a possum. We got out of the truck and the kids came over. I thought they were going to sniff us like dogs. They looked to be about eight, ten, and twelve under all that dirt, the boys being the oldest.

Leonard said, "Aren't y'all supposed to be in school?"

The oldest said, "We're off today."

The girl said, "We don't go much. Daddy said we're gonna start getting home schoolin'."

In what? I thought. Collecting dirt?

"Haskel around?" Leonard asked.

"He's out to the barn," the oldest said.

"Could you go get him?" I asked.

The older boy studied me. "Well, I reckon."

"I mean, if it wouldn't hurt you," I said.

"I don't reckon it'll hurt none. Y'all stay right here. Pa don't cotton to folks wandering around here much."

"Probably afraid they'll step on a nail," I said. "Or trip over a car part. Or maybe step in a possum."

The kid went away then, but not like he was in a hurry.

Way he walked with his head down, you might have thought he was cataloguing worms and insects in his path.

The remaining two kids stared at us. The little boy looked to have caught a good shot in the forehead at one time, maybe with a stick or a rock. He had a crease there, like you might iron into a pair of trousers. The little girl had black greasy hair with lovebugs in it, patches of dirt on her face that gave her a spotted pup appearance, and slimy trails from her nose to her upper lip.

I tried to make small talk with the kids, but they didn't exactly warm to me. They didn't seem annoyed either. Sort of ambivalent, as if they had both just gotten over a lobotomy operation and were still weak from it.

Fifteen minutes later the oldest boy came strolling up. He said, "Pa's comin'. He told me tell y'all you better not be sellin' nothin'."

"We're buyin'," I said. " 'Course, if he wants a good set of encyclopedias, we might can fix him up."

"I wouldn't count on it," said the older boy. Then added proudly: "He don't read much."

I looked up then. Coming around the far side of the house was a man I assumed was Haskel. Even from a distance, you could see he was about as clean and cuddly as a steaming pile of diseased dog shit. He had on a pair of faded overalls with no shirt, and was spitting a nasty brown stream of what I hoped was tobacco.

He walked briskly, and as he neared I could see he wore a pair of loafers without socks, and the arms that swung by his sides were big and gnarly, as if they had been broken several times and the bones had healed improperly.

When Haskel was still out of earshot, Leonard said, "Let me do the talking."

Haskel walked up, wiped his hands on his overalls and

put them in his pockets. I could see his right hand had hold of something bulky in his overall pocket. I assumed it wasn't his dick.

Haskel looked at us carefully. He had a bumpy face that made you nervous. He said to Leonard, "I reckon I know you, don't I?"

"You have a good memory," Leonard said.

"Double-barrel shotgun, sawed off," Haskel said. "Some ten year ago."

"More like fifteen."

"More like twelve, now that I think about it. I ain't as good with colored faces."

"We all look alike, huh?"

"Far as I'm concerned, everybody looks alike, but coloreds look more alike. I hope you ain't working for the law now."

"Why would I?"

"Sometimes it happens. It's not something I like. I tend to become angry something like that goes on."

"Don't try and scare us," Leonard said. "It isn't necessary."

"There's lots of fellas weren't scared that aren't scared even now, but they ain't happy neither. They got dirt in their faces and they lay nearby."

"The garden?" I said.

"What?" Haskel said.

"You know, the garden," I said. "For fertilizer."

"You could talk yourself to death," Haskel said.

Leonard said, "Listen here, Haskel, that gun in your pocket, it'll only get one of us. Maybe. Then the other one will clean your clock."

I jerked a thumb at Leonard and said to Haskel, "Be sure you shoot him so I'm the one does the clock cleaning."

"You might find my clock hands harder to wind than you think, boys," Haskel said, then noticed his children standing around. The little girl had her mouth open and was picking her nose. The other two boys were watching Haskel as if waiting for him to offer them their medication.

"You goddamn kids run along to the house now," Haskel said. "Go squirrel huntin'. Fish. Make yourself useful. Don't make me tell you twicet. And get your fuckin' finger out of your nose, Sherilee."

The goddamn kids evaporated, though Sherilee kept her fuckin' finger in its probing position. Maybe it was latched there.

Haskel said, "Little shits."

"You always greet people want to do business with you like this?" Leonard said.

"I'm cautious," Haskel said. "You can't be too goddamn cautious these days. Consider what happened to those folks in Waco."

"You mean the religious nuts who were abusing their children?" I asked. "You know what I think, except for those poor children and the government folks, fuck 'em. Far as I'm concerned the only thing wrong with that operation was the government folks were stupid and the folks inside the compound were even more stupid. I figure you're that stupid, you ought not be in the gene pool."

"You're awful uppity for a man who's come to see me," Haskel said.

"How you know I'm not here to give you a Jehovah Witness tract?" I said.

Haskel turned to Leonard: "What can I do you for this time, colored fella?"

"Leonard's the name."

"I don't like to get too personal," Haskel said. "Fact is,

I'll tell you right now, I don't shake hands. Now. Later. On the deal. Anything. I don't like being touched. I ain't one for having fingers run through my curly hair, you know what I mean."

"And it's such lovely hair," I said. "Very gritty."

"What?" Haskel said.

"Forget it," Leonard said. "Don't pay him any mind."

"I tell you what," Haskel said, "you two jerk-offs get back in that there truck and haul on out of here. I don't like you much."

"We're not here to be friends," Leonard said. "Hap here, he got up on the wrong side of the bed this morning. Had to get rolling before he had his coffee and jerked his dick. But you don't like us, that's okay. You can like our money."

"Yeah, well," Haskel said, giving me a beady eyeball, "now we got that out of the way, you know what I sell, so let's get on with it."

"We need some cold pieces," Leonard said. "And not so old you load them with a ramrod and a powder horn."

Haskel was all business now. It was like we'd never had a disagreeable moment. "Heavy work?"

"Hard to say. We don't want machine guns, stuff like that. Simple, effective stuff. Probably close-range. One long-range weapon might be good. Maybe two."

"Cowboy style?"

"That's one way of putting it."

"Stuff like that, it doesn't come cheap."

"Let's see what you got, then talk prices."

"All right," Haskel said, then nodded toward me and asked Leonard: "This guy, he gonna have anything to say about this?"

"Jes when Massa Leonard say it okay to talk," I said.

"He jokin'?" Haskel said.

51

"Yeah," Leonard said. "He does that all the time. He thinks he's funny."

"Well, he ain't. In fact, I've already had about enough of him. Come on."

As we followed Haskel, Leonard cut his eyes toward me. I gave him a big juicy smile. It was nice to put Leonard on the receiving end of bullshit for a change. Guy like this Haskel, I couldn't help myself. Then again, it was me and Leonard buying from him, so what did that make us? Thinking about that, some of the humor went out of my spirit and my feet began to drag.

We went around the house, past some leaning sheds and a pen with hogs in it. The hogs came up to the fence and stuck their noses through and sniffed. The wind was picking up their scent, and I'll tell you, it was healthy.

Down past the pens and the outhouse, which had a unique and memorable aroma all its own, we entered a path in the woods, and after a while we came to a clearing, and in the clearing was a huge well-cared-for barn. Out to the right of the clearing were a number of stinking armadillo carcasses; nothing was left but the decaying shells and the ants and flies they housed.

There was a mound of dirt beyond that, and I could see something on top of the mounds, in a row, about two feet apart, but I couldn't make out what it was.

Inside, the barn was air-conditioned. Haskel flipped a switch and the lights came on and showed boxes and racks of guns and the smell of gun oil was strong and sweet, and there was the stench of gunpowder too, and it was acrid and biting to the nostrils. In the back you could see a kind of gun range with bags of sand and bales of hay and targets.

"Run everything on a generator," Haskel said. "Got to keep it a certain temperature for the stuff I carry. Not too cold. Not too hot. There's shit in here, weather got wrong, it'd go off and blow our asses all the way to Mineola. Maybe out in the goddamned Gulf."

"I don't like to travel that far unless I got plane tickets and a steward in my lap," Leonard said.

Haskel cut an eye toward Leonard. "You mean stewardess, don't you?"

"I don't think so," Leonard said, and let Haskel churn that one over. Haskel didn't seem to come to any decision. Maybe he'd look up the word "steward" in the dictionary after we left and think about it some and be real upset. I hoped so.

I was amazed at all the guns and ammo and the boxes that surely contained more of the same. On racks were things like rocket launchers and grenades and knives. I personally don't like the idea of someone as stupid as Haskel with guns. Actually, I didn't like the idea of anyone with guns. Me especially. It was one thing to own a handgun, a hunting rifle, but to have enough weapons to give the United States Army a fight went beyond desire for liberty and went over into plain ole anarchy. Pretty soon we would decide liberty also included the right to own our own personal backyard nuclear device. That goes with our right to bear arms, doesn't it? Maybe Haskel could sell us a nuke and we could use it to turn Tillie's new pimp into a mushroom cloud. That would teach him.

Haskel raised an arm and pointed around the expanse of the barn. "This has got to be the best goddamn store of weapons in East Texas. Maybe Texas. What I'm sayin' to you is, had I not done business with you before, colored fella—"

"Leonard," Leonard said.

"—I wouldn't be doing business with you now. If anything goes wrong, and things come back on me, and I get my dick in the wood chipper over selling you guns, I got connections, and these connections, they wouldn't like to find out you fucked me. You did that to me, even if I'm in a jail cell, some night you go to bed, you won't wake up. There's people I know will see to it."

"Wow," Leonard said, "I just had a little tingle all the way to the end of my big black toes. What about you, Hap?"

"My toes aren't black, but I think I felt a tingle."

Haskel said, "What I want you to do is go over to that table there, write your name on the pad, and I want you to show me your driver's license so I know you got the same name you put down. You got other identification, I want to see it. That way, something goes wrong, cops come down on my head, I got your name and identification. We all go down together."

"Last time I was here you just had guns in the trunk of your car," Leonard said.

"Business is good," Haskel said. "That Waco thing, the Oklahoma bombing. That's good for business."

We went over to the desk, got out our driver's licenses and let Haskel look at them. Neither of us had credit cards to show, but we both had ancient Social Security cards and we let him look at those. He carefully wrote down our license and card numbers and we signed the notepad.

I felt creeped by all that. Cops, FBI agents raided this place, there was my name, my address. Not only was I fucked, but so was Leonard. Once again, I had dragged him into the shit.

When we finished, Haskel went away for a moment, came back with an armload of weapons. He put them on a bare table by the door. He picked up one of them, a double-barreled shotgun.

"Apologies to you, colored fella, but they call this a nigger spreader."

"How nice," Leonard said.

"Twelve-gauge Remington double-barrel. Short barrels, not sawed but specially altered by yours truly. Short-range, hair triggers. Let this fucker go in a filling station shitter, it'll kill everyone in there, wipe their asses and flush the commode. Interested?"

"How much?" I asked.

"Eight hundred dollars."

"Goddamn!" Leonard said. "Sonofabitch better not just wipe asses, it better come on over to my house and suck my dick."

"It might do it," Haskel said, "but this baby sucks your dick, you won't like it. Shit, colored fella—"

"Leonard."

"—you was expectin' illegal cold guns to come at Kmart prices?"

"We were hoping," Leonard said. "I don't suppose that price includes ammunition?"

"It don't, but I'll throw in a box of shells."

"Two boxes of shells, and shave a hundred dollars off and you got a deal," Leonard said.

"Sold," Haskel said, and put the shotgun on the table and picked up a rifle. It was one of two. "My design. You want to cowboy, you get to cowboy." Haskel tossed the gun to me and I caught it.

It was a Winchester-style rifle, mid-length, with a loop cock and two barrels, over and under. "Unique," I said.

"Yeah," Haskel said. "I call it the Haskel 'cause I made the sonofabitch myself. Got a general Winchester design, and I put that loop cock in there 'cause it's easy and fast to handle. I always liked the old *Rifleman* show. He had one like that. John Wayne used a loop cock in the movies too. The shotgun idea I got from another show I used to watch. *Shotgun Slade*."

I turned the rifle over in my hands. I may not like them, but I know a good one when I see it.

Haskel said, "That baby holds twelve .44 cartridges, and underneath it has a shotgun shell. It's activated by that second trigger. It clicks back once, then sets, and you click it again. It's a twenty-gauge. It hasn't got the room-cleaning power of that Remington, but you get one man in your sight, let loose on him, and he'll be cool in the summer and cold in the winter.

"The top barrel is accurate, and it'll shoot a goodly distance. More than that middle-measure barrel will lead you to believe."

Haskel picked up the other rifle of the same design and tossed it to Leonard. "I'll even throw in a box of shells per rifle," Haskel said.

"Yeah," Leonard said, "but how much are the rifles?"

"A thousand apiece."

"Shit," Leonard said. "Maybe we ought to get a powder horn and a ramrod and a Hawking reproduction."

"I've got 'em," Haskel said. "Look, you take both, I'll make 'em eight hundred apiece. I'm actually selling these bastards at discount prices."

"Seven hundred apiece," Leonard said.

"Seven-fifty," Haskel said.

"Oh, all right," Leonard said, but you got to throw in one of those pistols."

Haskel looked down at the table. He had brought out three handguns. He picked up one of the snub-nose .38s and weighed it in his hands as if he could tell its worth that way.

"All right," he said. "But no shells with it."

"How much are the shells?" Leonard asked.

"Sixty dollars."

"For a box of .38s?"

"For twenty shells. They're all dum-dums."

"No thanks," Leonard said. "Plain ole .38s will do. We want to be prepared, but we're not trying to take on the Republican Guard."

"All right. Anything else?"

"Shit, Leonard," I said. "We don't need all this stuff. Lose the shotgun and one of the rifles."

"You never know," Leonard said. "Give us three hand-guns, provided they aren't a thousand a pop and my balls on a platter."

"You can keep your balls," Haskel said, "but the pistols, they're seven-fifty apiece."

"Jesus," Leonard said. "You have these cut out of you, or what? That's dear."

"Take 'em all, get a discount."

"How much?"

"Fifty dollars."

"Fifty dollars! Jesus Christ, you're really giving us the Jesse James."

"These prices are bargain-basement, man."

"Whose basement?"

"All right, I'll cut you a hundred on the deal. Throw in a box of shells."

Leonard sighed. He looked at me. I said, "I tell you, we don't need all this stuff. I'm a man of peace."

"Yeah," Leonard said, "but they might not be."

"You got you a little something planned," Haskel said. "A job."

"Nothing like that," Leonard said. "All right, wrap it up."

"Don't you want to see this stuff work?" Haskel asked.

"Yeah, well," Leonard said. "I reckon."

8

"We can go outside for these," Haskel said. "I use the range in back for the heavy shit."

Leonard and I each carried a rifle and Haskel carried the sawed-off and the revolvers and ammunition in a cloth bag. He walked us out the door, down the trail, and over near the hog pens. He put the bag down, broke open the double-barrel and took two shells out of his overalls pocket and pushed them into the gun.

"Watch this," Haskel said, and suddenly he turned toward the hog pen and cut down with both barrels. There was a sound like God letting a big one and the fence splintered. When the smoke and dirt and hog shit cleared, both hogs lay with their feet in the air.

"Goddamn," Leonard said. "Wasn't any call for that."

"Gonna eat 'em anyway," Haskel said, opening the shotgun and popping out the shells. "Soon as I get you two packin', I'll get my woman to help crank them sonofabitches up with the wrecker and we'll scrape 'em. Scrapin' a hog beats scaldin' any day. Still got to use lots of hot water, but it ain't quite the work. Come here, now."

We followed Haskel down the trail to a spot at the base of the barn. "Ya'll want telescopic sights for these?"

"No," Leonard said.

"Might ought to have 'em," Haskel said.

Leonard shook his head.

Haskel said, "See them bumps on the hill out there?"

We nodded.

He swapped his shotgun for the rifle Leonard was carrying.

"Watch this." Haskel jerked the rifle up and fired and cocked and fired in rapid succession. The bumps on the hill went away. "Come on out with me now," Haskel said.

As we walked we could smell yet another awful stench. It wasn't the outhouse and it wasn't the pigs; it was something long dead and rotting. It was more armadillo carcasses. They were spread at the base of the little sand hill, and at the top of the hill we saw what Haskel had been shooting. The heads off buried armadillos. We stood at the top of the hill, and all around the spots where the exploded heads stuck out of the dirt there were bones and fragments of skulls and brains, and down on the far side of the hill were wire cages. All but one of the cages was empty. It housed a frightened armadillo that kept darting from one end to the other.

"Were those armadillos alive?" Leonard asked.

"Ain't no fun shootin' a dead'n," Haskel said. "Fuckers root up everything. Figure this is how they pay."

"They're just doin' what their instincts tell 'em," Leonard said.

"Reckon so," Haskel said. "But so am I."

Leonard carefully laid the shotgun down, then I heard

the wind, but I didn't see the punch. It was a right cross, I think, and it caught Haskel on the left side of his cheek and it made a cracking sound, and Haskel seemed to leap away from the hill. He hit the ground at its base, rolled and lay on his face. I was amazed to see that the rifle Haskel had been holding was in Leonard's left hand. He had snatched the weapon and punched Haskel in less time than it took to spit.

Leonard raised his knuckles to his mouth and sucked on them. I went down the hill to see if Haskel was dead. I lifted his head up and dirt fell out of his mouth. I set him up, got behind him and pulled the little revolver out of his overalls pocket and gave him a couple of whacks on the back with the palm of my hand. He coughed and rolled his eyes.

"You fugger," Haskel said.

Leonard came down the hill and got out his wallet. He looked at me and sighed, took out the bills. There were a lot of them, large bills. Hundreds. I knew he had gotten them out of the bank for this gun buy, that it was a chunk of the money from the recent sell of his uncle's old house.

Leonard pushed the bills down the front of Haskel's overalls. "Here's the money for the weapons and ammo, shit-wipe. We'll pick them up on the way out. That diller in the cage down there, I've tossed in another fifty, so I'm taking him with me. Cage too. Any of your friends, or you, show up to bother us on account of this, I want you to know they're gonna miss all future meals. And I can find my way back here too, and I do, it won't be to try and sell you no vacuum cleaner. You happen to wake up when I'm through with you, it'll be with a tube in your nose and a shit bag strapped to your hip."

"Azoles," Haskel said, then stretched out on the ground and turned his head to the side and lay still.

I emptied Haskel's revolver, dropping the shells in my hand. I put the shells in my pocket and leaned down and put the gun back in Haskel's pocket. I picked up the cloth bag on my way away from there.

Leonard got the armadillo cage, carried it down the hill with one hand, the rifle in the other, the shotgun tucked under his arm. Down at the barn, we went inside and I got the notepad with our names on it and bent it in half and shoved it in my back pocket. We gathered up the guns and the ammo.

We went out to the truck. Leonard put the dillo in the truck bed. I stepped over the dead possum and got inside the truck with my weapons and ammo. Leonard went around and opened the driver's door and put the guns and ammunition he was carrying inside.

Sherilee, without her finger in her nose for a change, sort of materialized. She said to Leonard, "Ain't that our armadillo?"

"I bought him," Leonard said, closing the door and leaning against his truck.

"Pa traps 'em."

"Uh huh."

"Where's Pa?"

"He got a little tired. He's up on the hill there, resting."

"In the dirt?"

"He was sort of overcome with exhaustion."

"You hit him didn't you?"

"Yes ma'am."

"Sometimes he hits me. He knocked me out oncet with a shoe."

"Just consider that one for you," Leonard said, "and call it even."

"He ain't so bad sometimes," the little girl said.

"You ought to tell someone about the hogs. Haskel shot 'em."

"He does that sometimes," said the little girl. "When they get big."

"Well, they ain't gonna get no bigger."

"Reckon not."

Leonard gave the little girl a pat on the head and drove us out of there. When we reached the main road, we saw Haskel's two boys walking. They had cane fishing poles on their shoulders and sullen looks on their dirty faces. They didn't wave at us.

When we had gone a few miles down the road, Leonard pulled over to the side, got the cage out of the back of the pickup and walked into the woods, set it on the ground, and opened it.

The armadillo sat quietly, looking at the open space. Lovebugs buzzed around our heads and caught in our hair and clothes.

"Go on and git," Leonard said.

The armadillo did not go on and git.

Leonard picked up a stick and poked at the armadillo's rear end, but the beast didn't seem any more ready to leave. Leonard picked up the cage and gently poured the armadillo onto the ground. The armadillo landed on its feet and turned its head and sniffed the air. It appeared to be in shock, and considering what had happened to his relatives, I couldn't blame him.

"Now, you go on and stay out of trouble," Leonard said.

The armadillo moved slightly so that it stood next to Leonard's leg. It made a snuffling sound, as if smelling Leonard's socks, or maybe working up to a good cry.

Leonard picked up the cage, and we went back to the truck. When Leonard put the cage in the truck bed, we looked up to see the dillo had followed us to the edge of the woods.

"I've never seen anything like that," I said.

"No, me either. I reckon the little fella don't know he's comin' or goin'."

Leonard went around and got in the truck, started up, and drove off. I looked in the side mirror, said, "He's standing in the middle of the road."

"Dammit," Leonard said. He found a spot to pull around, went back and parked, got out and grabbed the cage. He opened it and set it on the ground in front of the dillo. The beast ambled into the cage and lay down. Leonard closed the cage and put the armadillo in the truck bed and got back behind the wheel, paused to pull lovebugs from his hair and toss them out the window.

"Damnedest thing I ever saw," Leonard said, rolling up the window. "Couldn't leave him though. He'd probably end up caught again, target practice for Haskel."

"Probably. Think Haskel is going to hunt us down and kill us?"

"You destroyed the record."

"Haskel could have memorized our names."

"Let him come see us, then."

"That was one hell of a punch you hit Haskel with."

"Actually, I must be getting old. Skin on my knuckles scraped worse than usual."

"Can you still get your pecker up?"

"I can hang an American flag on it and wave it."

"Then you're not getting old."

"What're you snickerin' about?"

"Your dillo."

"What about him?"

"Neat," I said. "You've got an heir."

9

Back at Leonard's house, Leonard took the dillo into the woods while I made coffee. He came back a few minutes later carrying the empty trap. I watched him from the kitchen window. I thought he looked a little sad.

I poured us coffee, took the cups out on the back porch. Leonard joined me and we sat on the steps and sipped. I said, "When do we leave?"

"Tomorrow morning."

"That's what I figured. That's what I told Brett."

"I think we ought to see we can take Brett's car. We'll need the trunk room."

"Done," I said. "She'll be glad to do it."

Leonard nodded. He said, "You want to back out, we can."

"I didn't say anything about backing out."

"I know, but I'm givin' you the room."

"I'm committed. I asked you to help me, remember?"

64

"I remember."

"If you want to back out, you can."

"You've had to bring a man down before, Hap, and you brood over it still."

"I'd hate for there to be a time I didn't brood."

"What we're doin' now ain't self-defense. We're goin' lookin' for trouble."

"I know that."

"You might have to kill someone."

"I know that too."

Leonard sipped his coffee, took a moment to study one of his fingernails. He wasn't looking at me when he spoke.

"There's things I can live with. Things even you don't know about. I'm not complainin', and I'm not apologizin'. I'm just sayin' there's things I can live with maybe you can't."

"Like killing people?"

"You got more bleeding heart in you than the whole Democratic Congress. You don't like guns. You're going against everything you believe because of Brett. You don't owe this to her. Me, if I know where there's a nest of poisonous vipers and I can stomp them flat, I think I ought to do it. I figure you'd feed the vipers, try to raise them up, maybe finance their college. I'm not saying one thing or another about this being wrong or right, I'm sayin' how you are and what you're goin' to be dealing with. If what the midget said is true, we got the Oklahoma mafia going on here. We're walkin' onto their playin' field, and we'll be expected to play. These guys, they take their money, their drug pushin', their pussy peddlin', and their murderin' seriously."

I sat silent for a while. Leonard took my coffee cup and left, came back with filled cups for us both.

"You're not altogether wrong, brother," I said. "But I love Brett. Brett loves Tillie. So I got to do it."

Leonard nodded. "Since you might stop in the middle of the action to pet a puppy dog, I figure I got no choice than to go in with you."

"You always have a choice," I said.

Leonard looked at me and laughed a strange laugh. "The hell I do."

I didn't know how to react to that. I eventually just looked away. Out at the edge of the woods, giving us a stunned look, was the armadillo.

"Your son has returned," I said.

Leonard looked up and saw the dillo. "Well, I'll be damned."

We drove over to see my boss at the Black Lace Club, which was essentially a big nasty honky-tonk on the outskirts of town where women shook naked titties on stage to bad country-rock music and sometimes slipped their briefs down to give the drunks a view of the squirrel in the tree.

Most of the time, this led to the dancers having money tossed at them or pushed into their panties, but other times it led to drunks taking it as an invitation to walk on stage and screw whatever was in front of them. That meant the girls, me, the manager, another drunk, the stage, whatever.

It was my job to see they didn't screw anyone, make too much noise, or fight each other over who could drink the most, had the fastest car and the biggest dick. It was a terrible place, a terrible job. In two weeks you could have more fights and nasty confrontations than three average persons had in a lifetime. It was one of the old-style bad places. Not the new places with clean floors and strobe lights and girls that looked as if they stepped out of the pages of *Playboy*. Not the places where the worst you had to deal with was some frat boy who thought he was tough. This was where the big bellies and the brainless collected. Guys that wouldn't fit anyone's idea of a stereotypical Hollywood tough guy, but the kind of guys who could take any one of those sleek, muscled-up ego machines and kick their asses until it bored them enough to stop.

I had come to feel working in this place was just helping it survive, and that was like feeding shit and sugar to disease-carrying flies. Why do it?

When I got there a couple of the daytime bouncers were on duty, and they knew me. They slapped me on the back and shook hands with Leonard when I introduced him. They were good guys, just shy on brains.

Day duty isn't so bad. Mostly married businessmen on business trips who had wives back home who had gotten fat. They come in for a drink and a look-see, and maybe later they could get it up enough to jerk off back at the motel.

My boss, Billy Joe James, was sitting at a table auditioning a new girl who was dancing pitifully to a tune playing on a cheap recorder. She had about as much rhythm as a stick. She didn't look bad, however. She was mostly ass, titties, and a dull expression. Looked about thirty, but a good thirty. She had a watery-looking tattoo of a red heart on her ass, and a red and blue tattoo that might have been a parrot, but could have been most anything, on her ankle.

Billy Joe saw me and Leonard, smiled at us. He waved the girl from the stage. She came down the steps like her feet hurt, which considering a large part of her outfit was a pair of tall red high heels, was likely. The rest of her had on a red G-string that was mostly up her twat.

When she came over to Billy Joe's table, he said something to her and slapped her on the ass. She shrieked like it was all in good fun, grabbed her shirt off his table, and went away. She passed us, pulling on her long shirt, and the expression on her face told me she wasn't having any kind of fun at all.

We went over and sat at the table and Billy Joe smiled at me. Billy Joe had a fat face any mother would love to hit. Many times. He said, "You ain't come for money, I hope."

"Actually, I have."

Billy Joe nodded, wiped fingers through his oil-slicked brown hair. "Figures." He looked at Leonard. "How's it goin', Pine?"

"It's goin'," Leonard said.

"You know I don't pay nothing until Saturday morning," Billy Joe said. "It's always Saturday mornin' that I pay."

"Well, you know," Leonard said, "right now, it's bound to be Saturday mornin' somewhere in the world, don't you think?"

Billy Joe laughed a little, not like he thought the joke was all that goddamn funny, but like maybe a good yuk might take some of the seriousness out of Leonard's looks.

"I got a little emergency here," I said. "And I'm quitting."

"Quitting? You can't quit."

"I just did."

"Oh, shit, man, you're my main bouncer. You can't quit."

"Just said I did."

"You can't."

"I believe you're not listenin' to the man," Leonard said. "Sounds like he's quittin' to me."

"Shit." Billy Joe looked at Leonard. "What about you, Pine? You lookin' for work?"

"Not here I'm not."

"You got a rep too. You're one hell of a bouncer."

"Not anymore. I've given up that profession. That and rose field worker and lay preacher are no longer on my résumé."

"I pay pretty good, and hey, you get to look at a lot of titties."

"I've seen titties and they don't interest me much."

"You some kind of fag?"

"Actually, I am."

Billy Joe studied Leonard for a moment. "Yeah. Really?"

"Really," Leonard said.

Billy Joe looked at me. "You and him? You know . . . you and him?"

"Only if my latest relationship with a female doesn't work out," I said. "Then, I got to consider it. I might even consider some bestiality. Come on, Billy Joe. I need my money and I need it now."

Billy Joe nodded. "All right. But you decide you want to work again. Or you want to work, Pine. You come see me, okay? It don't matter to me you're queer. No offense. You know what I mean."

"Yeah," Leonard said. "I know what you mean."

"We want to bounce," I said, "you'll be our first contact."

Billy Joe pulled a wad of cash from his pants pocket, counted out the bills as if he was pulling each one from his intestines. I took my money and we left.

Out in Leonard's truck, Leonard said, "Now I know why

you take a long hot shower every mornin' you come home from work."

Back at Leonard's I packed a suitcase, went into town to see Brett. I took her out to dinner on some of my money, told her our plans, then we went back to her place, sat on the couch and shared a nonalcoholic beer.

I told her about Haskel and the guns, about Leonard and the armadillo. I showed her the notepad with Leonard's and my names on it I had taken from Haskel.

I took the pad over to her sink and set fire to it. We talked while it burned on the porcelain. When it was finally all gone, I flushed the ashes down the drain and turned on the garbage disposal. Brett got us another beer, and we sat on the couch and passed it back and forth.

"What time tomorrow?" Brett asked.

"Leonard will be by about nine. We'll leave his truck here, load our guns and suitcases into your car, and start out."

"I'm a little scared," Brett said.

"I can understand that, but there's no need for melodrama. What we'll do is follow the address the midget gave us, see we can find Tillie, and if we can, we'll take her home. I don't think there'll be any real trouble."

"You're saying that to make me feel good."

"I really don't think there will be any real trouble, but like I said before, that doesn't mean it's going to be easy. But, it'll be okay. We might have to pop somebody's nose, but that'll be the extent of it."

"Promise?"

"No. I'm not that stupid."

Brett packed her suitcase, then we got naked and went to bed. The hair on Brett's mound, as we who read erotica like to call it, had begun to grow back. Mounting her was kind of scratchy, but being incredibly tough, I went ahead with the screwing anyway. Real men don't whine over scratchy female pubic hair. We just get on with it.

Fact is, I was so tough, I made love to her three or four times.

Consequently, when the alarm went off at eight the next morning, I felt like six pounds of runny shit that had passed through a goose and been washed down-country by a flash flood. Brett opened one eye, looked grim, said, "Oh, dick."

"Not right this moment," I said. "He's tired."

Brett whacked me. "That doesn't even interest me. I love you, but right now I could maybe marry anyone got me a cup of coffee."

I didn't get her a cup of coffee.

She didn't get me one.

We lay there for another ten minutes. "All right," I said. "On the double, we get up."

We got up, but not quite on the double. We showered together, made love in the stall, then showered again. By the time we'd dried off, brushed our teeth, and dressed, Leonard had arrived.

We gathered our suitcases, locked the place, and met him outside. We loaded the guns, which Leonard had wrapped in blankets, into Brett's trunk, tossed the suitcases on the back seat. Brett let Leonard drive. She sat between us on the front seat and we started out.

"See your son anymore?" I asked Leonard.

"He rooted up the place last night. He was sleeping peacefully under the porch this morning. I've decided to name him Bob."

"That certainly took some strain," Brett said.

"I get enough strain without trying to cleverly name an armadillo," Leonard said.

71

We stopped at Burger King, bought some breakfast and lots of coffee, then headed for Oklahoma, minding the speed limit, minding our manners, minding our business, praying for hope, expecting rain.

10

We got on 59, headed north to 259, caught I-20 at Kilgore and went west toward Dallas. We skirted the roof of Dallas, hit 35, and except for a couple of pee breaks, we rode it all the way into Oklahoma.

We stopped at Ardmore about eight that evening and had dinner in a steak house. When we finished, we decided to find a place for the night and smoke on into Hootie Hoot early in the morning.

We got rooms at a cheap motel and toted the blanket-wrapped guns into the rooms with us, just in case someone decided to steal a spare out of our trunk and ended up with a bargain.

Brett and I had a small room that smelled strongly of detergent or disinfectant, but after brushing our teeth and washing our faces, we found the bed inviting and the smell less annoying. We didn't feel like making love, which meant we were probably on our way to a solid relationship. We just slept together, cuddled up spoon style.

When we awoke the next morning it was raining lightly. We collected Leonard, had breakfast at the same cafe where we had eaten our steaks, and set out again. The rain began to fall harder, and the storm followed us all the way into Hootie Hoot, which lay about twenty-five miles outside of Oklahoma City.

When we got there, it was early afternoon and the rain had not stopped. Hootie Hoot was, as Red had said, a burg. There was a long street with old brick buildings. A theater, a cafe, a filling station, and, strangely enough, a taxi stand, with one old battered blue cab out front. I wondered where it took people. Up one side of the street and down the other?

We didn't see any neon signs that blinked BIG JIM'S HOOTIE HOOT WHOREHOUSE, so we left town and found another cheap motel five miles out, not far from I-35. Leonard got a room next to ours. We bought some groceries at a little store across the highway, sat in Brett's and my room laying out plans and eating store-bought ham and cheese sandwiches and Cheez Doodles.

Leonard finished his lunch, sat by the window. He held a can of Coke in one hand, held the curtain back with the other and watched the rain snap down on the parking lot. He said, "Thing is, whatever we do, we got to do it and be done with it."

"My suggestion is we find the whorehouse and start from there," I said.

"Now that's a good idea," Leonard said. "I'm glad you're along, Hap. Me and Brett might not have thought of that."

"Do we just go in and get her?" Brett asked.

"I don't think that'd work so good," I said. "Posing as a customer is probably the best way to go."

"And you'll have to be the customer," Leonard said.

"You think they'll know you're gay?" Brett asked.

Leonard laughed. "No, but they'll know I'm black."

"Oh," Brett said.

"Black or white may not matter," Leonard said, "but this is a little burg in Oklahoma. I was in Maine, I'd be thinking the same thing. It might not matter, but on the other hand it might. My guess is this is a redneck operation."

"Remember what Wilber said about Big Jim being nice to niggers," I said. "That doesn't bode well for Brother Leonard here."

"No use getting the rednecks stirred we don't have to," Leonard said.

"That doesn't sound like you," I said.

"Older and wiser," Leonard said.

"So you'll go in?" Brett asked me.

"Yeah," I said. "Thing we got to do next is find the whorehouse, and, as Leonard pointed out, maybe I ought to do the investigation work on that instead of him. They might not take kindly to a brother askin' where the white women are."

"Couldn't some of the women be black?" Brett asked.

"They could," I said, "but in redneck mentality it's okay to screw a black woman, but it isn't okay to have a relationship with her."

"And it isn't okay at all a black man screws a white woman," Leonard said. "Weird territorial stuff."

"And there's another thing," I said. "We don't even know there's a house of ill repute here."

"Ill repute?" Leonard said. "Man, you been reading those Victorian novels again?"

"Red could have lied," I said. "In fact, this is all starting to look like a big joke on us. He might not even have worked for any Big Jim. There might only be one grain of truth to the story. He knows your daughter works as a prostitute, and maybe he knows that because he was a customer."

"The old postmarks on Till's letters were out of Oklahoma City," Brett said.

"Yeah," I said, "a card mailed from here, most likely that's where it would get stamped. But it's all iffy."

"I'm prepared for it not to work out," Brett said. "But I'm more prepared to do something. It makes me feel like I'm trying."

"I'll start now," I said.

11

By the time I drove Brett's car back to Hootie Hoot, the rain had slacked and the little town looked better than before. It hadn't suddenly grown in size and had a Wal-Mart SuperCenter built out to the side, but it was shiny and nostalgic-looking.

It made me think of one of the cozy little towns my mom and dad had lived in briefly while my father worked as a mechanic for an oil and gas company. It was very Andy of Mayberry. Clean and simple, where everyone knew one another, and maybe minded each other's business too much, but where most of that business would be about little more than a secret apple pie recipe. And, of course, the location of the local whorehouse.

I pulled in at the taxi stand and got out. The stand wasn't much of a place. A little building made of brick that might at one time have been some sort of store, or maybe even an old jail.

Inside, slouched down in a plastic chair next to a card table, was an older man with a three-day growth of tobacco-specked gray beard. His feet were stretched out, resting in another chair. A TV, festooned with rabbit ears wearing aluminum foil accessories, was perched on a little stand next to the wall. The TV was playing only static. But that was all right, the man in the chair was asleep.

There was a dusty calendar on the wall above the TV. It bore a winter scene with snow-covered trees and a sled and two kids in coats, wool hats, and fat mittens. The calendar read December 1988.

There was a small refrigerator in one corner of the room, and I could hear it humming, as if to entertain itself. It was a sound that made you sleepy.

There was a stack of worn paperback Westerns on one corner of the card table. One of them was open and turned facedown.

Next to the book was a cold-drink bottle full of tobacco spit with a fly on the bottle lip and one inside too stupid to find its way out. It kept buzzing around, hitting the glass, but it never went up to the opening. The sky was the limit, but it was too dumb to know.

Finally the fly, pissed off, flew down and sat on a tobacco chunk in the bottom of the bottle, floated there on its nasty little island amidst an ocean of brown spit. It beat its wings a moment, as if to pass the time. Eventually, it stopped doing even that. Just sat there, confused, surprised, a real loser.

I sympathized.

The fly on the bottle lip, fed up with the ignorance of its comrade, flew off.

I stood watching the man for a while, trying to stare in such a way that his primitive brain would pick up my signals. I was attempting to activate that supposedly dormant sixth sense we all possess but so seldom use.

Either he didn't have a sixth sense or I was missing mine. He didn't move.

I knocked on the table.

The man opened his eyes and looked at me. "What do you want?"

"Well, I'm at a taxi stand. Say I wanted a taxi?"

"What for?"

"To go someplace."

"What I mean," said the old man, dropping his feet from the chair and sliding them under the table, "where would you be going?"

"That's a good question. And I have an answer."

"Yeah, well, good. Take this chair and sit in it while you tell me."

I pulled the chair around in front of the table and looked at the fella. He appeared to be very tired, and maybe not as old as I had first thought, but certainly no spring chicken.

"Let me tell you something," he said, "this here is a taxi stand, but I don't really do much taxiing. I take Old Lady McCullers into Oklahoma City twicet a week and do some shoppin' for her. I got a few more customers I do similar things for, though they ain't as excitin' as she is. She has a gas problem. I have to drive with the windows down all the way there. She don't even say excuse me or nothing. I look back at her in the rearview, she's lookin' at me like I cut 'em."

"So what you're saying is you drive gaseous old ladies around, but you won't drive me?"

He leaned and looked past me, through the glass, at Brett's car. "We gonna hook up your car and pull it?"

"Yeah, well, that would be a problem, wouldn't it?"

"What you really want?"

"Oh, just curious about a little taxi stand like this. In a town like this."

"Nothing else to do on a rainy day, so you just drive off I-35, come in here to talk to some local color?"

"Something like that."

"I think you're full of shit, mister."

"Well, I could use your rest room, you got one."

"Right back there, and don't make a mess of it. I don't normally allow customers back there."

"Maybe you ought to," I said. "That way they won't fart in your taxi all the way to Oklahoma City."

He laughed a little. "You might have a case there," he said.

I went to the rest room, took a leak, washed my face, studied it in the mirror. It looked as tired as Mr. Taxi Stand's. I went back and took my chair.

"Haven't had enough charm for one day?" he asked. "Here, let me give you the five-cent story. Hootie Hoot used to not have I-35 out there. That was long ago. Used to be three, four little towns around here next to us. They weren't real big, but they were bigger than we were. With one taxi I had a little business. Enough I could take care of my family. Towns around us died, and this one's dead and don't know it.

"You drive down the road a piece there, take a right first real road you come to, and you'll go through a burg used to be three times this size, but it ain't nothing now but empty buildings with the store glass knocked out by vandals. I hang on here 'cause I ain't got nothing else to do. Wife died. Kid got married and lives in Tulsa. Me, I got a little war pension and a few bucks now and then from the farting lady and a few others, and it's all I need. And I got a feeling you didn't come in here 'cause you needed no taxi. I got a feeling you didn't come in here 'cause you were curious how come Hootie Hoot's got one."

"You could be right. By the way, what's with the town's name? Hootie Hoot?"

"I've heard about twenty stories," he said. "Not one of 'em worth a shit and none of them interesting enough for me to repeat, and I don't think you really care one way or the other."

I nodded. "All right," I said. "I got a real reason. I thought as a taxi driver you might could help me with something. I'm looking for a place. A house of prostitution."

"Ah," the man said. "I should have known that. I'm losing my snap. It's just I don't get many drop-ins for that. Mostly they know where they're goin'. How come you don't?"

I studied him. There was a lot more going on behind those slow brown eyes than waiting for the Channel Nine weather report.

"I was just told it was here in Hootie Hoot."

"Ah hah. Where you from?"

"LaBorde, Texas."

"Ah. Texas. You drove all the way from Texas to Hootie Hoot, Oklahoma, for a good time at a whorehouse? What's the deal? They don't make pussy in Texas no more?"

"I wanted to be real private."

"I don't think you wanted to be hundreds of miles private. I think you, sir, may still be full of shit. Even if you did go to the john."

I considered for a moment, took a flyer. "All right. I'm going to tell you straight."

"That's good."

"I came here because the woman I care about has a daughter who's a prostitute and she wants out, and a guy

81

told us this is were she is. Me and her, and a friend of mine, we come here to find her and take her home."

"So you ain't after pussy?"

"No. Well, I mean, not that way."

"You want this gal from the whorehouse?"

"If she's there. I don't even know she's there. I don't even know there's a whorehouse."

"You don't know much, do you, boy?"

"Frankly, I don't."

The old man rummaged around in his shirt pocket and came out with a nasty-looking hunk of a chaw. He chewed off a bite and worked it around in his jaw and studied me for a while. He got up and turned off the television set. He went over to the little refrigerator and got out a soft drink and twisted the top off, said, "Want a CoCola?"

"Yeah," I said. "That would be nice."

He pushed the drink toward me and I took it. He picked up the soft drink bottle with the fly in it and spat down the bottle neck, splashing the fly off its island and into the nasty brown ocean. He shook the bottle and watched the fly go under.

We sat that way for a while, me sipping a Coke, and him chewing and spitting into his bottle, shaking that fly around in the spit. He said, "You found this whorehouse, what were you going to do?"

"I told you that."

"But you didn't say how. Let me tell you somethin'. This house you're lookin' for, it exists. It's down the road a piece. There's busloads come to that house. It's out in the sticks 'cause it don't bust up no big laws out here. That's the way they like it around here. They want stuff like pussy shacks out of sight and out of mind. There's people drive from Oklahoma City just to drop their goodies there. There's conventioneers hit that place on the way to Okla-

82

homa City and back from. It's busy. And it's not a casual kind of place neither. Least it ain't if you really know how to look around."

"I'm not sure I follow you."

"The guys run that place, they ain't just big thugs, they got guns. They're not going to take kindly you takin' one of their whores. I think they might twist your arm behind your back, make you yell calf rope, then break your arm off and stick it up your ass. Then they might shoot you and bury you under a rosebush somewheres."

"That's what my buddy thinks," I said. "And I'm starting to believe it. The view seems to have a consensus of opinion."

"But you're going in anyway?"

"Yes."

"This ain't no daughter of yours?"

"No."

"This woman whose daughter it is ain't your wife?"

I shook my head.

"This gal ain't no stepdaughter?"

"Nope."

The old man shook his head. "I hate them pimpin' sons-abitches. I ain't got nothing against pussy, and I reckon some gal wants to sell it, that's her business, but this place ain't so cut-and-dried. I think a gal wants to leave, they don't just let her leave. I think she wants to go, they ought to let her go. It ain't the pussy sellin' bothers me, it's the lack of free will."

"I take it this place has been here a while?"

"Many, many years. Used to be run by a madam named Lilly Filigree, and I think most of the girls there chose to be there then, and from what I know, she treated 'em good. When I was a young man I went up to there myself, rode a little tail up the canyon oncet or twicet. But now, last ten years or so, it's just business. All business, and it ain't the girls' business."

"Anyone ever tried to close the place down?"

"Oh yeah, back when there were enough people in this town to fill a church, a bunch of self-righteous old biddies tried to shut it down. Mostly 'cause their men were up there getting their ashes hauled now and then."

"They didn't have any luck?"

"Sheriff, he kind of slapped the madam's wrist now and then. Ran some of the girls in around election time. But it didn't mean nothin'. But it's not that way now. Not just a bunch of ladies makin' a buck for a fuck. Folks run that show, they ain't sweet. Used to be a colored lady up there ran it. She came after Filigree. She was as mean as a goddamn crocodile. Seen her a few times in town. Always wore this big old sack dress."

"A muumuu," I said.

"You say so. She went away and there was a cowboy midget and a big bastard runnin' it. Midget liked to come to town so people would look at him. Strutted around like a banty rooster. Right proud of himself, he was."

I thought about Red and his expensive Western-cut suits. I thought about the lady in the muumuu, resting in a box at the bottom of some lake in Arkansas. Maybe still in the muumuu, shit-stained as it was.

Taxi Man spat into the soft drink bottle, said, "Figured that midget and ole bigin' was runnin' things. Then they were gone too and there's a fellow up there now scares me just to see him come into town and sit in the barbershop. He don't even pretend he does anything other than sell pussy. But hell, there ain't nobody 'round here cares. This ain't where he gets his action. It's them conventioneers and such pay his bills."

"I see."

84

"No you don't. You go up there and fuck around, and that monster gets hold of you, they gonna find you in some rock quarry with a .44 slug behind the ear."

"Cheery scenario," I said.

"Not really."

"Any chance you're going to tell me where this place is?"

"All right," he said. He produced a stubby pencil from his pocket, wet it with his tongue, used it to draw a map on the fly page under the title of one of the paperback books. I thanked him, took the book, put it in my back pocket.

"Had any balls, I'd go with you," he said.

"It's not your problem."

"Things like this ought to be everyone's problem."

"I guess."

"Maybe if I was younger."

"Sure."

I started out the door and he called out, "Hey, boy, you watch your ass."

"Thanks," I said.

12

At the motel I told Brett and Leonard what I had learned.

Brett said, "I don't get it. Everyone knows it's up there. This taxi man, he says he knows the girls are sort of prisoners—"

"Sort of," I interrupted. "Tillie got into this by choice. This is the sort of business you don't know who you're going to end up with. Not just in bed, but in business. One day you're selling your product and paying a percentage. Next day you're owned and selling your product and you get a percentage, and sometimes maybe the customer gives you a black eye. A disease."

"But the cops?" Brett said.

"There's one local cop," I said. "He probably makes more money a year than all the whores do, and he don't make it on law enforcement."

"So they get away with it," Brett said.

"Yeah," I said. "And the place has a reputation almost like a landmark. Kind of a hangover from the past. Lot of people think, well, they're just sellin' meat, what's the problem?"

"So," Leonard said, "the next step is?"

"Way I see it," I said, "is I could go up there now, pose as a customer and try and take Tillie out. But I think it's better we wait until tonight. That way, I pull it off, we can hustle her out of town with some dark to help us."

Leonard nodded. "That sounds all right. You go in there, though, you go in with a gun. I didn't haul all these weapons down here for nothing."

"Actually," I said, "I hope you did."

"You know what I mean," Leonard said. "I'm going to be nearby, and not with any handgun neither."

I looked at Brett. She sat quietly, churning her own thoughts about.

Shortly before dark Leonard and I walked down to the Coke machine next to the motel office. I put coins in the machine and got myself a Diet Coke, Leonard a Dr Pepper, and Brett an orange drink. I gave Leonard the Dr Pepper, slipped Brett's can into my coat pocket, pulled the tab on the Diet Coke and drank some of it.

"How do you think Brett's doing?" I asked.

"I don't know," Leonard said. "She's hard to read."

I looked out at the highway. Leaves were being blown downhill by a sharp cool wind. The gold and red and brown leaves whirled and whipped above the highway in the fading sunlight like dying birds, floated down and stuck to the cement. Cars came by and tossed them up again. It began to sprinkle gently.

"You watch her," I said.

"I will."

We went back to the room, drank our drinks, and I read some of the Western Taxi Man had given me. Leonard paced, went to the bathroom numerous times. Brett lay still on the bed. Once when I looked at her and smiled, she looked at me as if I were nothing more than the nasty wallpaper behind me. It made me nervous.

It went like that for another hour, then the daylight faded. I closed up my book. Leonard handed me the little .38 and I put it in an ankle holster and strapped it on and pulled my pants leg over it. Leonard stuck a revolver under his shirt and gave Brett one. She looked at the pistol with an expression that was hard to figure. Maybe she was thinking about Tillie. Maybe she was thinking what I was thinking. I was scared.

Brett slipped the gun into the holster Leonard provided, strapped it on under her coat. Leonard rolled all the big guns back into the blankets, except for the double-barrel. He held it up and looked at me. "Honky spreader."

We gathered up our goods. Leonard carried the shotgun down close to his side. It was raining when we went out. We put the gun-stuffed blanket in the trunk, tossed the luggage in the back. Leonard put the shotgun with the luggage. We stopped up front of the office, and I went in and checked us out of the motel.

In the car I got out my flashlight and opened up the paperback Taxi Man had written on. I studied the map and told Leonard how to go. The rain pecked at our windshield and the wet leaves slapped against it and tangled in the windshield wipers, wadded, and were tossed away.

We drove on into Hootie Hoot. Up Main Street and past the taxi stand. I tried to look and see if I could see Taxi Man at his post behind the card table, but it was dark and the street was poorly lit and it was raining hard now.

On up the street we went, out of Hootie Hoot. The rain

began to die. I studied the crude map inside the paperback, and we followed it to a blacktop road that turned right. We took it, went along on that for five miles, then turned left on another blacktop. This one was narrow and wound down amongst scrubby Oklahoma trees wound tight with darkness and nesting crows.

We went along the blacktop for ten miles and the trees broke on either side and there was a great hill up ahead and the blacktop quit there and turned into a gravel road, and at the top of the hill the half moon, which had finally shone itself through fading rain clouds, seemed to be balancing, like half a loaf of round white bread, on its rim.

We kept going. Down on the other side the hill fell away into a wide pasture and in the center of the pasture was a big old white house. It was well lit from the inside and by porch lights, and on either side of the house by two tall pole lights that shone on the pasture and revealed it was full of cars and rain puddles.

The house was three stories with columns and a long wide porch that wound all around it. It had a new roof sprouting four brick chimneys. One for each side. All four were breathing smoke. You could see the smoke against the moon, which now sat just above the house like some kind of soiled halo.

"Business is good," Leonard said, and stopped at the bottom of the hill and rolled down his window and spat outside. He took several deep breaths. I could hear music coming from the house, and I could hear some laughter and some other sounds. It seemed to be a raucous place.

"Well, brother," Leonard said, "what's the score?"

"Park far out. I'll walk."

"And when you come out," Leonard said, "I'll be too far away."

"I know. But they see y'all sitting out in the car, it'll make them wonder."

"You're trying to say these boys may not like niggers?"

"You said it first, remember."

"I tell you what I'm gonna do," Leonard said. "I'm going to give you the time to get down there. Then I'm gonna give you fifteen minutes to line up things, like you've come to shop. Then I'm going to move on down about halfway and park. I'll be on the right. Where you see the gap in those cars. That's where you want to head. You're not out of there in twenty minutes, or I hear some kind of hootenanny goin' on, I'm comin' in."

"That'll just cause more trouble," I said.

"Not if they're gutting you with a knife," Brett said.

"I guess that's a point worth considering," I said.

I got out, started walking toward the house.

The wind gathered up the scent of incense and passed it on to me. It was a nice smell. Any other time I might have appreciated it. The music was country. Tanya Tucker. It was cranked up so loud it seemed to be responsible for the leaves blowing off the trees.

When I was on the porch, a guy big enough to fill a bus and stick his ass through the door came outside and made the porch creak when he walked. He was wearing a dark suit with a white shirt and a dark tie. He had a head about the size of an atlas globe and his hair was cut so short, in the porch light I could see razor scrapes on his blue-veined head. He smiled at me.

"Hello," he said. "Come on in."

"Thanks."

He walked down the porch, around it, out of sight. Inside was a brightly lit foyer, and the music was really loud. Tanya Tucker was over with and some guy whose music

I didn't know was singing about something I wasn't listening to. Loud as that music was, it wasn't as loud as the thumping of my heart, the pounding of blood in my temples. The incense was so strong in the foyer it made me sick.

A woman in her sixties, carrying about two hundred pounds, and not carrying it well, wearing a multicolored, loose-fitting dress that had all the style of a horse blanket, sort of sprang up in front of me. She had blue hair and loose dentures and too much powder and rouge on her face. She looked as if she ought to be somewhere else, baking cookies.

She said, "Young man. You come for a good time?"

I hesitated, fearing she might think she was supposed to be my good time.

"Yes, ma'am, I suppose I have."

"Well, there's a small cover charge. Any other charges, that's between you and the girls."

I realized then she was a door greeter, sort of like they have at Wal-Mart. Need a shopping cart? Want to buy some pussy? Man, that was cold. A sixty-year-old woman to warm you up. Like Grandma guiding you around on your first day at kindergarten.

"How much?"

She told me and I gave her some of my bouncer money.

"You need to come into the sittin' room, son. Look around. See if there's anyone you like. The girls are real friendly."

I went past her, through a half-open door and into the sitting room. It was busy in there. Lots of men, all white, were sitting on couches and lots of girls were flittering around them, as if the men were magnets and they were flecks of iron.

91

The men's talk was loud, to compete with the music, to try and not show nervousness. I figured there were plenty of husbands in here who weren't regular whoremongers, but who were trying to start out in style. Most of the men in the room looked to be either businessmen or farmers, and all but one looked to be past thirty.

The women were all young and looked to be whores, of course. You could tell from the lack of clothes. I checked each one individually, trying to determine if any of them were Tillie. Well, maybe that wasn't why I looked so carefully, but it was part of the reason.

Over by the crackling fireplace was a Steroid Jock wearing an expensive hand-tailored suit, but that didn't make it pretty. He had chosen to have it made out of a kind of olive green material the texture of grape leaves. His head was square, like a block, and it was topped with black hair cut close to the scalp. His ears reminded me of radar tracking devices. He was talking to a handsome blond man in another hand-tailored suit, only this one was blue and smooth and more tasteful. Then again, who was I? A fashion critic?

The guy in the blue suit was huge too, but it didn't show right off, he was so well proportioned. I realized utility instead of fashion had more to do with the hand-tailored suits these guys wore. You looked like they did, you couldn't pick a suit off the rack. The guy in the blue suit was watching me, like a bird stalking a worm. He had one hand on the mantel and he was playing with a smoking pot of incense.

I glanced around the room and saw more of the boys. Not the customers. Just these big sonsabitches. They were trying to look casual, but they looked about as casual as warthogs in jockstraps and snowshoes. There were six of them altogether, packed into those expensive suits, housing enough steroids inside their flesh to accommodate the entire Mr. Universe competition. I wondered how many more like them were upstairs. I thought about the one on the porch. Maybe he and Leonard were sitting on the steps right now, talking about the moon.

Naw.

I took a deep breath and put a smile on my face and started walking among the women, like I was shopping. A redhead looked at me and smiled. Bless her heart, I'd seen more sincerity in the grin of a presidential candidate.

I grinned at her, just to be sociable, but tried to discourage her by turning away and looking at my watch. Only problem was I wasn't wearing one.

How long had I been inside now?

Five minutes?

Ten?

Soon, Leonard would be moving the car closer, and not long after that he'd be inside looking for me.

I turned slightly and the redhead was at my shoulder. She wasn't gorgeous, but she was cute. She had a lump of a nose, good teeth, and freckles to go with the red hair, which was the color of copper and probably that way naturally. She was a little thick in the hips, but if she'd been wearing more than thin black panties that wouldn't have been noticeable. Another ten years those hips were going to give her trouble.

She had me by the elbow. She said, "You need some company?"

"Well, I'm looking for somebody."

"Here I am."

"I'm looking for someone named Tillie. I hear good things about Tillie."

She frowned. "You don't hear good things about Darlene?"

"Well, I don't hear bad things about Darlene. It's just I'm looking for Tillie."

"I don't know any Tillie."

I tried to remember the photograph I had seen of Tillie in Brett's house. "She might go by Till. Something like that. She's a redhead too. Big-breasted."

"That's it. You don't like me because I have small tits."

I knew she could care less if I liked her or her tits. She was doing what she was supposed to do. Drum up commerce.

I saw her glance toward the fireplace mantel a couple of times, looking at the guy in the blue suit. He glanced at us, then looked away, checking out the rest of his business. And I was sure it was his business. Or at least the one he was running for Big Jim. I figured he was the big guy Taxi Man had told me about.

"About this Tillie?" I asked.

"There's no one named that here," she said.

"Not even upstairs?"

"You really want this Tillie, don't you?"

"I'd like to try her. I've heard good stuff."

She shook her head. "Sorry, no Tillie. You get bored and I'm not playing the horizontal tango with some redneck's weasel, you look me up. For two hundred dollars I can make you forget Tillie, or damn near anybody or anything."

"I'll remember that."

She winked at me, went to join a couple of guys who had just entered the room, and they were damn glad to see her. One of them instantly had his arm around her, and I heard her laugh like she had just heard the funniest goddamn joke ever told.

Time was running out. Already Leonard was slipping

shells into that double-barrel. Beard the lion in his den, I thought.

I went over to the guy in the blue suit. I said, "There's a girl I'm looking for. A Tillie. She here?"

The guy studied me. The guy with him, Cement Head, studied me too. "No," he said. "There used to be a Tillie here, but she's not here anymore."

"Where'd she go?"

Cement Head said, "She ain't anywhere close. If you want loving tonight, Tillie's out."

Blue Suit turned his head and looked at Cement Head. There didn't seem to be any expression on his face, but there was certainly an expression on Cement Head's face. Fear.

Blue Suit turned back to me and gave me a smile. His face didn't go along with the jock build. It was very suave and assured. Here was a man who didn't have to pay for pussy and knew you did.

"There's plenty of girls here can do it for you," Blue Suit said.

A log shifted in the fireplace, crackled. I jumped a little.

"Nervous, aren't you?" said Blue Suit.

"My first time in a whorehouse," I said.

He smiled, "Well, we sure wouldn't have figured that."

Cement Head laughed on cue, but didn't overdo it.

Blue Suit said, "That little redhead you were talking to can do more tricks with your dick than a monkey on a jungle gym. My advice is you latch on to her. Though it looks like she'll be occupied for a while."

I looked to see her going upstairs with a man on her arm. He was feeling her ass and she was smiling like there wasn't anything better in the world to her than a strange man's hand up her crack.

"She's good," Blue Suit said. "I promise you that. And they don't come any cleaner."

"She's got that new car smell, then," I said.

He smiled at me. "That's right. She may not be new, but she smells new."

I gave a good leer and went back into the crowd. I wasn't sure what to do next, but the next moment, a lot of decisions were made for me.

Through the half-open door came someone I knew.

He was wearing an expensive-cut gray Western suit, little gray boots with red jalapeños stitched onto them, and he had on a white ten gallon hat big enough to cook chili in.

It was Red, the midget. Beside him was Wilber, wearing a neck brace. First thing they saw as they entered was me.

13

A lot of things went through my head right then, but none of them told me why the midget and Wilber were here. From what they'd said their lives were on the line and this would be the last place they should be.

But there they were, standing just inside the door, looking at me as if they had just sighted the Virgin Mary in see-through panties and high heels.

I think it took the midget a moment to put it together, but I could tell Wilber knew who I was right away. His mouth fell open and his eyes widened. I believe he and I were mirror images at that moment.

Wilber reached down and got hold of the shoulder of the midget's suit, trying to alert him, but there was no need. Red had figured it out. Wilber bent down and Red said something in his ear, then smiled at me. Red walked behind one of the couches and over toward the fireplace.

I stood there a moment, trying to decide what to do. One thing was certain. The pickle was out of the jar.

I started walking slowly toward the door, hoping Wilber would let me pass, and knowing he wouldn't. I tried to go wide to his right, but he said, "I don't think so."

I didn't hesitate. I kicked out hard and caught Wilber in the thigh with the toe of my shoe. It was a good shot, right where the muscles group, and he let out a grunt and bent over. I shifted slightly away from him and snapped my foot up in a back hook and caught him with my heel in the face as he was bent. I made a run for it then, but one of the big guys in the hand-tailored suits appeared. He was so large that when he stood in front of the door it disappeared.

I faked by raising my hand, and he looked up, and I kicked him in the balls, trying to make a field goal somewhere in Central Texas.

It was a good ball shot, but either this guy had nuts of steel or had used so many steroids his 'nads had gone to seed, because all he did was make with a grunt and come at me.

I couldn't deal with his size and strength, so I tried to sidestep, but I bumped up against somebody, one of the girls, a customer, whatever, and he hit me with a glancing right that jolted me so hard the coins in my pants pocket changed denomination.

I tried to hit him back, but found it hard to do from the floor. And besides, the ceiling was falling on me.

Or so it seemed. It was No Balls coming down on me, and he had hold of my coat and was lifting me. He drew back his fist. At that moment I was so stunned, I sort of welcomed any blow he might give me, but there was still enough reflex in me, still enough of the fighter, that I responded by poking my fingers into his eyes.

He barked, dropped me. I rolled against someone, tried to get up. But the someone was Wilber. He hooked his arm over the back of my head, under my neck, had me in a guillotine choke. I stomped his foot and grabbed one of his legs behind the knee and broke his balance while I swatted his balls with my free hand hard enough for them to replace his Adam's apple.

He let me go and I squatted and struggled for the revolver in my ankle holster. About that time the door swung wide and there was an explosion and plaster rained down from the ceiling like snow.

I glanced up, and there was Leonard holding the double-barrel, one barrel displaying smoke and sending out a gunpowder stench that temporarily masked the incense in the room.

No Balls had recovered again, and he wasn't afraid of a shotgun. Or was too stupid to know what it was. He charged Leonard. Leonard sidestepped, swung the double-barrel and hit the big bastard so hard that guy's distant relatives must have jumped in their chairs.

The big man struck the door behind Leonard, slamming it closed, knocking out the bottom panel with his head. He tried to pull his head back through and Leonard banged him with the barrel again, this time across the ribs, then pointed the shotgun at the other muscle guys who had stupidly made a knot over on the left side of the room. All except the guy in the blue suit and Cement Head, that is. Cement Head was standing in front of Blue Suit, ready to take whatever might come, and Blue Suit was calmly looking over his guard's shoulder.

Red, wearing his stupid ten gallon hat, was standing next to him, close to his hip, watching the events.

I shouldn't have, but I looked at Wilber on his hands and knees, trying to get up, and was overcome with rage.

I swung my foot in an arc and brought it down on the back of his neck brace with a snapping motion. Wilber screamed, hit the floor and lay there holding his neck. "That hurt! That hurt! Oh, God, that hurt!"—like maybe it was supposed to feel good.

"Well, Hap," Leonard said. "Looks like you've shit in the porridge again."

"I'll say."

I pulled my ankle gun and backed toward Leonard. The big guy with his head through the door was trying to pull it out again. Leonard let him this time, then rapped the barrel over his head harder than ever. The big guy decided to lie down and rest for a moment, but I could see he was twitching already, working to get up.

Leonard opened the door and we backed through it. I heard the sound just a little too late. It was the man I had encountered on the porch. He was rushing our backs like a missile.

Leonard wheeled, cracked the bastard's head with the barrel of the shotgun, then kicked out and knocked him down. The man came up with a gun in his hand, and Leonard, casual as an angler casting a fly rod, jerked the shotgun down from where it lay over his shoulder, and fired. The man's left foot went away and he fell to the floor and thrashed like a chicken. Blood went everywhere. Leonard leaned over and casually picked up the man's pistol and dropped it in his coat pocket. He said, "From now on it's all left shoes for you, Bubba."

Leonard broke open the shotgun, put the discarded cartridges in his pocket, and reloaded. He might have been doing nothing more than looking at a splinter in his hand, he was so blasé.

The door in front of us was wide open now, and gradually the bodyguards were sliding into the room. They had guns. No more tackle and punch shit. They were going to kill us.

Red pushed in between their legs, for all the world acting like a kid who was about to see something neat in a peep show. Leonard snapped the shotgun shut. We all jumped, then froze.

There was a sound behind us. I glanced carefully over my left shoulder and saw Brett enter the room. She was carrying a pistol by her side. The old lady who had invited me to have a good time came after her, as if to claw her. Brett turned and swung the pistol against the old woman's head like she was burying an ax in a log. The old woman went down on her knees and dropped her dentures on the floor and held her blood-spurting forehead, said, "You stinkin' cunt." Or so I believe. It was hard to tell without her teeth.

Whatever it was, Brett didn't like it. She bent down and struck her again, this time behind the ear, not hard, but solid enough. The old woman hit the floor, rolled and cussed and bled all over the carpet.

Brett walked up between us. I said, "Let's back out."

I thought all the guns in the room would go off then, but they didn't.

Leonard shouted, "I pull this trigger, half the room disappears."

That got everyone's attention. Maybe that's what they'd been thinking all along and that's why no one had done anything. There's nothing like a shotgun with barrels big as subway tunnels to make you take time to consider.

"All guns go away now, or I pull the trigger," Leonard said. "Do it!"

A couple of beats as everyone looked at the guy rolling around on the floor, screaming, clutching his ankle, his foot spitting blood. The guns went back inside suit coats.

"You," Brett said to the midget. I turned my attention to the front of the room.

Red pointed at himself.

"Yeah, you," Brett said. "Shit pile in a hat. Get over here, you little cocksucker."

Red looked around for help. No one was offering any.

Leonard said, "Do as the lady says, or you're gonna be even shorter."

Red wandered toward us, like an amnesiac man who had just walked free of a plane crash somewhere in the Yucatan. In the doorway I saw Wilber appear, one hand on the neck brace. He looked at me with fire in his eyes.

"How's the neck?" I said.

The fire in his eyes turned to lava.

I gave Red a quick pat-down, found a revolver under his coat. I put it in my coat pocket. I put one hand on Red's shoulder, and we started backing. Brett deliberately stepped on the old woman's hand as we went. The woman bellowed and her teeth, which she had recovered and replaced, flew out again. Brett kicked them across the room, and we kept backing. We backed like that all the way out to the car. The entire gang, bodyguards, whores, and johns, and the old woman who was constantly gumming cuss words, came out on the porch and stood under the porch light looking at us.

Leonard opened the trunk, told Red to get inside.

"You've got to be kiddin'," Red said.

"I look like I'm in a humorous mood?"

"I can't stand tight places."

"You think the grave ain't tight?"

Brett grabbed the brim of Red's hat and jerked it down over his eyes. She whapped him a good one on the top of the head with the pistol. "Do what he says, dick-lick!"

Red hesitated almost as long as it takes to skin the

wrapper off a stick of gum, then, the hat still over his eyes, he got hold of the car, climbed inside the trunk, and Leonard closed it.

Leonard gave me the shotgun, went around, got behind the wheel and started the engine. Brett slipped into the back seat. I slid in on the front passenger side, closed the door, and stuck the shotgun out the window.

We roared out of there so fast Leonard fishtailed and banged Brett's car into the side of a pickup truck. But that didn't stop us. With the moon at our backs, we went up and over the hill and away, rattling the midget and the guns in the trunk.

14

"I don't like it," I said.

"Doesn't matter what you like," Brett said.

"Leonard?"

"It's rough, Hap, but far as I'm concerned, it's the way to go. Little shit nearly got us all killed. We got to profit from him."

We had found a road out in the boonies and Leonard had pulled off, hoping to lose any pursuers we might have gained. If anyone had followed, we hadn't seen sight of them yet. Maybe they were thinking about the shotgun. Then again, Leonard had been driving almost seventy miles an hour on roads that were designed for thirty, so there was a good chance he lost them before they could find their car keys. His driving had been almost as scary as our time in the whorehouse.

We were standing outside the car, beside the road in the bright moonlight, about to open the car trunk. Brett wanted to pistol-whip the dwarf into talking, and Leonard was for it too. He and Brett were just trying to decide on the best pistol for the job. Brett favored a long-barrel, and Leonard thought a short one was better because you could use it up close, requiring no more effort than the snap of a wrist. I didn't know we had a long-barrel, but somehow Leonard had come up with one of those too, a cold piece from his closet.

I didn't like the idea, short barrel or long. I was trying to talk them out of it. It's one thing to hit a guy in self-defense, another to deliberately pistol-whip him.

"Just enough so he talks," Brett said. "Then maybe a little for entertainment."

"I don't know," I said.

"We came all the way up here because he said my daughter was in trouble. Then we see him here. What he told us, it could mean anything, Hap. We could wine and dine him and give him a cigar, but I figure a pistol-whipping is a lot quicker and it would certainly make me feel better."

"That's the part worries me," I said.

"We didn't come here to be nice," Brett said. "You're the one told me it might not be pretty, and now you're trying to make it pretty."

"I'm trying to be human. Revenge isn't the way."

"People say that just ain't never had call for any revenge," Brett said. "Besides, I just want to loosen his tongue some."

"Yeah," I said. "Till it falls out of his mouth."

Leonard rapped on the trunk with the shotgun, which I had returned to him. "Hey, turd. I'm gonna open this trunk, and if you've got one of those guns in there, I want you to know, all the ammunition is in the suitcases in the back seat, so don't waste your time. Besides, I fire in there with this shotgun, we'll be puttin' what's left of you in your hat and still have room for your clothes and a pound of shit. Hear me?"

"Yeah," said a mumbled voice. "But I don't want to be pistol-whipped."

"Been listenin' have you?" Leonard said.

"Yeah," Red said. "This guy, Hap, you call him. He's right. You ought not take your anger out on me."

"Who says I'm angry?" Leonard said. "I just like to watch a midget take a beatin'."

"You and everyone else," Red said.

"I'm gonna open the trunk now," Leonard said, "and when I do you better roll out of there pretty. You don't, I'm gonna cut down on you."

Leonard twisted the key in the trunk and hopped back. The trunk lid flew up and Red's hands appeared over the edge. "Don't shoot," he said, and came out of there with his cowboy hat crunched down on his head, his eyes barely showing beneath the brim.

"Come over here," Leonard said.

Red sighed, sauntered over to him.

"You want it with the hat on, or off?" Leonard said.

"What a choice," Red said.

"The hat would cushion it some, but it'll get all bloody."

"This is a Stetson," Red said, "they're expensive." He took it off and straightened it out and lay it on the ground, sighed, stood in front of Leonard. "Maybe we could talk before you start hittin'?"

"I ain't hittin' shit," Leonard said. "Least not yet. She's doin' the work."

Red studied Brett. She was walking toward him with the long-barrel revolver held by her side. Walking like a woman with a mission.

Red looked at me. "You don't want her to do this. Stop her."

"I don't like it," I said, "but you talk, you won't have to have it."

"Talk about what?" Red said, and suddenly Brett was there. The pistol went out and caught him alongside the head and dropped him. When he went to his knees, Brett whipped the pistol back, got some skull with it, whipped it again, like she was trying to cut a Zorro Z.

Red fell face forward and groaned and tried to rise up on his hands, but he wobbled and went down again. "Oh, Jesus," he said. "I didn't think it would hurt that bad."

"Hell," Brett said, "I haven't even got my swing yet."

"Hold it, for Christ's sakes," I said.

I went over and got hold of Red and tried to pick him up. He said, "I think I like it better on the ground. I'm gonna take a beatin', least I won't have to keep gettin' up."

I let him go. Brett said, "You told me my daughter was here."

Red shook his head, and I saw a moonlit glob of blood fall out of his bright hair onto the ground. "I said she had been here and might still be. I didn't say she was definitely still here. I never said that. You, Hap, you were there. I didn't say that, did I?"

"Reckon you didn't," I said.

"What I want to know is where she is now," Brett said, "and if you're smart, you'll tell me while you've still got teeth to talk around."

"Maybe I ought to sit up," Red said.

I got hold of him and helped him to his feet. I walked him over to the car and opened the front passenger door. He sat down, his feet hanging outside the car.

"Damn, Hap," Leonard said. "Why don't you give him a pillow and a soft drink?"

Brett said, "Maybe I should hit him some more, just for grins."

"That's enough," I said.

"It's only enough when I say it's enough," Brett said.

"Goddammit!" I said. "That's enough!"

Brett gave me a look I didn't like.

Leonard said, "He don't talk, you can hit him some more, Brett. I promise."

I looked at Leonard. "I don't want it to come to us finding out who's the toughest, brother," I said.

"Me neither," Leonard said.

"Then I advise you not make loose promises."

Leonard grinned at me. I turned back to Red.

"Red," I said, "I want you to tell your story, and boil it down to the essence. Tell it straight. We got questions, you answer them, quick like. You've caused us trouble. I'm past irritable myself. I'm damn near sick with this mess. You fuck around, we might all have pistols and a need to swing them. Hear what I'm saying?"

Red nodded, used his hand to wipe away a trail of blood that was flowing from a pretty deep cut across his forehead, a cut made from the sight on the revolver.

He said, "I knew y'all were folks would beat a midget."

"I might kick a puppy, it bit me," Leonard said.

Red made a grunting noise. "I believe you would, mister."

"My whippin' hand's gettin' itchy," Brett said. "Talk, or your brains'll see moonlight."

"Ah, a line for the movies," Red said. "Save it for when you write your life story, lady. They pick it up for film, they might even let you play the part."

Red bent forward and let blood drip off his head and onto the ground. When he sat up, he was pressing his fingers against the wound. He said, "I told you how me and Wilber had our problems with Big Jim, and how we left out of here on our way to Mexico.

"Well, me and Wilber started to have a change of heart

about the time we got near the border. It was shortly after Wilber strong-armed a diner owner and cook, a Mexican. I, on the other hand, took money from the cash register and stayed away from that sort of thing, which I not only prefer not to participate in, I prefer not to witness. I only engage in violence when it's absolutely necessary and the money's right."

"Would you get on with it, you windbag?" Leonard said.

Red nodded. "So, Wilber, having just told the man how much he liked his steak ranchero, reached out and got hold of him, dragged him over the counter, and commenced to kick him. I should say, however, that the steak ranchero really was good, and that sort of bothered me. Eating a man's cooking, bragging on it, then beating him like he stole something. I've eaten in some of the best Mexican restaurants in the United States and nothing quite prepared me for the fineness of his steak ranchero. It was the sauce as much as anything else that made it special, though I believe the meat was of an excellent quality."

"Fuck the steak ranchero," Brett said.

"All right, all right," Red said, holding up his hand. "I'm a man who likes to tell a story complete. You never know when little details might matter. You might drive through that part of Texas at some point and want a good steak ranchero. I think the man will probably recover. It was a good beating, but I've seen people take worse and be able to function in time. So, he'll probably be back to cooking eventually. It behooves a person to pay attention to almost anything. You never know when something can be of use to you. I can give you the name of the place if you want it."

Brett said, "You know, you really are an idiot."

"Personally," Red said, "I believe that's a prejudicial statement directed toward my size."

"Your head's same size as anyone else's," Brett said. "It's the brain in it that's questionable. I'm going to ask you one more time. Where is Tillie?"

"I'm coming to that," Red said. "We took a car from the diner man, and as we neared Mexico it struck me quite soundly that I really didn't care for south of the border that much. Everything's different down there, and frankly, my whorehouse Spanish is nowhere as good as it once was. You don't use it, you lose it. And Wilber, well, if you want someone kicked around and hammered, he's your man, but public relations, that's out. And public relations in Spanish, well, that's certainly out. The only Spanish he speaks is on the menu at Taco Bell, and he has to read that off the card. I had to order the steak ranchero at the diner for him. He thought it was a ranch hero. Some kind of steak sandwich."

"You just can't lose that steak ranchero, can you?" Leonard said, and leaned on the car as if exhausted.

"So," Red said, "we're down South Texas way, and we start to consider our options, and this whole thing with Mexico, well, it's not pulling my string and Wilber isn't fond of it either. I decide we should call Big Jim in Tulsa. I tell him that I'm sorry, and that I did skim some money, but I also remind him that I made him a lot more money than the previous operator had been making him. I made promises that if he took us back we'd do right by him. So, he lets us come back. Not as managers of the whorehouse, but as drones. Working our way up again. He's quite forgiving, actually. I admit I thought he might shoot us both, but a life on the run, living off crackers, having to manage some kind of peanut operation in Mexico where it's hot as hell on a griddle, and where they speak Spanish faster than a calculator clicks . . . well, it was less than alluring.

"Case like that, sometimes you have to toss your hat over the windmill, so that's exactly what we did. Big Jim let Wilber and me come back. We robbed a doughnut shop in South Texas of three thousand dollars and two dozen glazed, ate the doughnuts and used the money to catch a plane, flew on into Oklahoma City where Big Jim had a party meet us, and not with paper hats and party favors either."

Red thought for a moment, as if sorting out details. "We were given a bit of an adjustment. A punishment, I suppose you might call it. I had to take a pretty good ass kicking. Literally. Numerous boots to the posterior, and I'll attest to the fact that the gentleman administering the kicks was quite good at it. My butt is still sore. But, I took my medicine and got it over with.

"Wilber, on the other hand, resisted a bit, so they hit him with an axe handle across the neck, necessitating the brace. But, after that, Jim took us back into his graces. It was that simple. He forgave us. I must say I miss our former position of authority and wealth, but frankly, I'd rather start all over again with Big Jim than be down in Mexico trying to run a string of Mexican whores or a dice game out of the back of a greasy filling station. And one thing about Jim, he may be a pimp and a crook, but he has a sense of honor sorely lacking in some of our public servants."

"Great," Brett said. "Now we know what you've been doing these past days, like we give a shit, but you still haven't said about Tillie."

"Tillie," Red said. "Yes. I was coming to that. She's gone."

"That's it?" Brett said. "Ten minutes of your crap to tell us she's gone? Gone where?"

"After I began to feel alert from the butt kicking, and Big Jim welcomed us back into the fold, he told us we were all heading for the whorehouse. He wanted Wilber and me there. My thoughts were that in time he was going to turn the operation back to us. Though, as Wilber has pointed out, sometimes I can be far too optimistic. We drove from Oklahoma City out to the whorehouse this morning with Big Jim. He even allowed that Wilber and I might partake of the products there, so, until your arrival, I was feeling very good. As if things were back on track. Wilber and I had just come back from Winston, a little town between Hootie Hoot and Oklahoma City, having gone there for dinner without any sort of escort or threats. We had a couple of steaks and came back, ready to relax, drink a bit, and perhaps, if the customers slowed, to partake of the female delights. Then your ugly faces showed up."

"Big Jim?" I said. "He was the guy in the blue suit?"

"Yes," Red said. "He was merely visiting. The guy standing next to him is actually the manager now, and I believe I should make note here and now that he's not all that bright. Honest, because he's stupid, but bright he isn't. If his brain was a battery it wouldn't give enough energy to fire up a penlight. Beside him Wilber is a mental gargantuan."

Red took another moment to bend over and let blood drip off his head, onto the toes of his boots. Looking at him there in the moonlight, so small, the blood flowing like that, falling onto those little boots, I felt sick and sorry and sad. My father and mother hadn't raised me to beat up midgets with pistols, nor to stand by and allow it to happen. I felt much smaller than Red, even if he was a cold-blooded killer and a windy sack of scum.

"It's bad enough you came in there like that," Red said, "but you stirred Big Jim up personally, and he doesn't cotton to thugs off the street tampering with his operation or running away with his personnel."

"I think maybe Big Jim might be led to think you were

in on our arrival," Leonard said. "I think he could be led to think that real easy."

"Now, wait a minute," Red said. "Why would I do that?"

"Could be that's what he's wondering," Leonard said. "Maybe he's thinking you linked up with us, and were getting back into his good graces to run some kind of scam."

"What kind of scam?" Red said. "What could I possibly gain?"

Brett cocked the hammer back on the pistol and put the gun to Red's head. "This is it, short stuff. The moment of truth. Where's Tillie?"

Red rolled his eyes toward the gun barrel, said, "Seems, that as punishment for helping me, Tillie had to service most of Big Jim's bodyguards. Except for Franklin because he seems to have trouble getting it up. He claims it's a psychological ailment, but we all know he takes too many steroids."

"We don't care about Franklin and his dick problems," Leonard said. "For heaven's sake. I'm going to have a nervous breakdown here. Will you just tell us where Tillie is?"

"Good-bye, shit sack," Brett said, and pushed the revolver hard against Red's temple.

"Tillie was passed around, then sent to The Farm," Red said.

"What's The Farm?" I asked.

"Ever heard of the Bandito Supremes?" Red asked.

"I take it that isn't one of the orders from Taco Bell," I said.

"Certainly not," Red said.

"Banditos are a Texas biker gang," Leonard said. "They're known to be in the drug business. The whore business. What have you."

"No," Red said. "Not the Banditos. The Bandito Supremes. They're bikers too, or some of them are, or were. But they're not even associated with the Banditos. They consider those guys sissies. They've fucked tougher guys than the Banditos behind the Catholic church. Could you take the gun from my head, lady? It makes me nervous."

"It should," Brett said, and eased the hammer down and pulled the gun back.

Red let out a deep breath. "The Bandito Supremes are modern Commancheros. Survivalist Nazis. Mostly they travel about, but they have headquarters in South and Southwest Texas, and Mexico. They have a farm, or what they call a farm, not far across the Mexican border. They do some work for Big Jim now and then. At certain types of work they can't be beat."

"I have a feeling that the work they do at this farm isn't about growing vegetables," I said.

"You are most correct," Red said.

15

After we got Red's story we sat around and thought about it awhile. As is usual with Leonard and me, we couldn't think of anything clever. We either needed to do it or not do it.

Brett had just one thing on her mind, of course, and that was go for it, with or without us. That meant we could leave her to her fate, or we could go along. So there was really only one actual alternative. Head for Mexico and The Farm.

Brett gave Red an ultimatum. Either take us there or end up a maggot hotel. Red, being the practical sort, decided to be our guide once we got into Texas.

We hit some back roads, and finally broke out toward Amarillo, Red riding in the trunk. All the time we drove I hoped the little bastard wasn't getting carbon monoxide fumes, and every so many miles I made Leonard stop so

I could check on him. Each time I opened the trunk and asked Red how he was doing, he'd give me a little wave.

Finally Brett and Leonard wore out with that method and moved Red into the back seat next to me and replaced his position in the trunk with suitcases. Brett rode up front with Leonard, and for most of the trip to Texas the two of them talked about country music. Red even had some opinions. He seemed to favor the Roy Acuff era and thought the rock sound was fucking up country music and he didn't like the way modern country and western singers danced around on stage. He thought they ought to just sing and go to the house.

One thing about Red, he was highly adaptable.

We arrived in Amarillo late that night. The town stank of slaughterhouses and stockyards. The air was absolutely thick with it. Sometimes breathing was like snorting a cow turd. It made me a little ill.

We stopped just outside of town and put Red in the trunk again, the suitcases in the back seat. Red was resigned by now and crawled inside without complaint, curled up next to the spare tire like a child crowding in close to his mother. He held his hat to his chest like a teddy bear.

We rented a cheap motel, because it had become part of our nature to do so, parked close to our rooms, and carried Red and his hat into Leonard's room with the guns and the luggage.

Inside the place looked pretty much like every other cheap motel room we'd rented. I felt as if I was in an episode of *The Twilight Zone*. Like no matter where I went, I ended up in the same room.

Leonard went out then, came back about a half hour later with some groceries, a bottle of aspirin, and some children's Band-Aids with Superman on them.

Red took about six aspirin and chased them with a Coke. I dabbed his bloody forehead with toilet tissue, slapped on a few Band-Aids. I stuck a wad of toilet paper to the head wound under his hair and left it there to dry.

"This is the sort of thing we have to deal with," Red said.

"What?" Leonard asked.

"Little people. We deal with this all the time."

"Getting pistol-whipped?" Brett asked.

"Abuse in general. And humiliation." Red turned his focus to Leonard. "You thought of getting me Band-Aids, you immediately thought of children's Band-Aids because of my size. You don't take me seriously because I'm small."

"They were on sale, asshole," Leonard said.

"I take you seriously," Brett said. "I pistol-whipped the shit out of you, didn't I?"

Red shook his head. "You just don't get it. None of you. Hap here, he might understand some, but ultimately, he goes with the flow. He's not a man willing to follow his heart."

"Were you following your heart when you strangled that woman who ran the whorehouse?" I said. "If you did do that."

"Oh, I did it. But that had nothing to do with heart. That was business."

"Consider this business," Brett said.

"Are you getting paid?" Red asked.

"No," Brett said.

"Then it's not business," Red said.

"I think it is," Brett said. "In fact, I think it's very serious business. And let me add this. I don't find my daughter, you're all out of business. Know what I mean?"

"Of course I do. Being small doesn't mean I'm stupid. Nor does it mean I'm physically inadequate. Would you suspect I can bench-press two hundred pounds? I may not look it in these street clothes, but I'm well muscled. Perhaps this isn't the thing to say in front of a lady—however, considering your actions of earlier, the idea of you being a lady might be questionable, so I think I can say it, and will. I have a big schlong."

"How nice," Brett said.

"Yeah," Leonard said, "but you have to climb up on a chair to use it."

Red was infuriated. "How much can you bench-press?"

"I don't know," Leonard said.

"I bet it isn't much for your size. You consider my size and the fact I weigh far less than two hundred pounds, and you're talking about me moving some real weight."

"That's good," Leonard said.

Red began to snort and rattle on about this and that. After about fifteen minutes of nonstop bullshit we had had enough. Leonard decided to gag him, and I helped. We used a pair of Leonard's underwear to do the job. We tied the drawers in place with a belt from one of Brett's dresses. Then we tied Red to a chair with a lamp cord and one of my belts.

When we were finished Leonard gave Red a pat on the head, said, "Just be glad them ain't Hap's drawers."

Brett put Red's hat on his head. Red shook the chair by rotating his hips and kicking his feet.

"You turn that over, I'm gonna leave you there," Leonard said. "You'll be damn uncomfortable lying on your side tied to a chair. You settle down there and after a while I'll let you loose for a pee break, otherwise you're gonna be miserable. And remember this, you ain't got no extra clothes with you if you mess yourself. Though, I suppose tomorrow morning I could run over to the children's department at a thrift store and pick you up some short sets."

Red quit kicking. His little shoulders slumped.

Leonard turned on the television. There was a rerun of *America's Funniest Home Videos* on. Leonard picked up Red's chair and sat him right in front of the television set. He took the Western novel Taxi Man had given me and stretched out on the bed and began to read.

"Well, that television show is our cue to depart," I said.

I glanced at Red: he had his head hung, defeated. On the television the audience was laughing as a toddler fell over the edge of a plastic swimming pool and banged his head against the ground.

Brett and I went to our room, carrying our little bit of luggage.

"I bought him some aspirin, didn't I? Paid for it out of my own money."

"Jesus, Brett. You hit him in the head with a gun barrel. A piece of steel. Aspirin doesn't make it okay."

"Well, aspirin's for a headache ain't it?"

"You gave him the headache. And besides, you gave Leonard a couple dollars and sent him for the aspirin."

"It don't matter how the little fucker gets it, does it?"

"I guess not," I said.

"He's lucky I didn't give him a new shape to his head. And don't be so self-righteous. You were in on it."

I went quiet. We were lying in bed, the light out. We were both well on our sides of the bed, leaving quite a space between us.

Brett said, "I'm sorry, Hap. Really. I shouldn't have said that. Wasn't for me you wouldn't be involved. But you got to understand. This is my daughter we're talking about.

Whatever it takes, that's what I'll do, and it's not like we're dealing with the Pope here."

"I know, Brett, it's just seeing the little guy take it. Fact is, I kind of admire him."

"Admire him?"

"Not for who he is. Or what he's done. But just the way he conducts himself."

"That prattling?"

"No, that drives me shit-crazy. But he has a sense of honor. Strength. Dignity."

"Next thing you'll be asking him to bench-press two hundred pounds and show you his pecker."

"I didn't say I liked him. I said I kind of admire him."

"I'll have to think about that one, Hap. You're pitying him, not picking up on a sense of honor. I've done the same, so I know. I'm an expert at recognizing the difference between admiring someone and pitying them. You have some of my old personality."

"How's that?"

"You see someone that's down, maybe not even someone you like, someone who's got a fucked-up life or who's taken a wrong turn, and you want to set them straight. You think all you got to do is get them on their feet. It's like the woman who takes up with the sorry man because she thinks she sees something in him, thinks she can change him."

"I know Red's worthless," I said.

"I'm not saying you're taking him under your wing and feeding him worms, but I'm saying what you feel for him is pity and it comes out of the same urge as the woman who wants to change the sorry man. You feel pity because he's a midget, or a dwarf, or whatever he is, like being small alone makes him worth a damn. He'd be sorry if he was eight feet tall. He'd be sorry if he had a nub dick and

120

couldn't pick up five pounds. He'd be sorry if he had a dick long as a rock python and could bench-press a gorilla carrying a sackful of coconuts. He might be sorry in a different way, but he'd be sorry."

"He was sold to a circus."

"There's people been sold to circuses that didn't grow up to strangle people over money. He admitted to robbing that diner while his partner whipped up on that poor man who cooked the steak ranchero."

"Boy, that must have been some steak ranchero," I said. "Way he kept talking about it."

"Yeah," Brett said, "and I'll be honest. I started to ask him where the place was."

We both laughed.

Brett said, "So you got to accept this guy isn't worth the powder it would take to blow his ass up. Lice on the end of a dog's dick have more sense of community than he does. He's out for himself."

"I know that."

"I know you know that, but you got to *really* know it. Between my husband and you I took up with this guy lived in a shed. I mean that literally. A shed. He conned someone to let him live in their shed. He wasn't even a particularly interesting, smart, or attractive guy, but he had a way of making you feel sorry for him. Sort of like an ugly mongrel puppy that had caught on fire and wasn't nothing but bald spots and red meat. You just naturally wanted to help him. He was a piece of shit, and I met him and got hung up with him, and I let him come over to the house cold nights and warm his pecker."

"I don't think I want to hear this."

"You know I wasn't celibate before we met. I never claimed to be any goddamn nun."

"Yeah, I know, but I like to think in a little fantasy compartment of my brain that you've been saving it just for me."

"You and a lot of others."

"Boy, that makes me feel good."

"I thought this pity I felt for him was love. I gave him money. I gave him chances. I took him out of the shed, and pretty soon he's lodged in my house tighter than a stitch. He wouldn't work. Not really. He'd piddle here and there to pick up a few bucks, but I never knew him to put in a full day's work once. He liked a good three hours and then back to the TV set, or he'd set around and play his harmonica and lie about how he used to play with Janis Joplin and Jimi Hendrix. Always had plans and opportunities just around the corner. He had a truck he borrowed that he was supposed to buy, and he drove it around for months, dodging the guy who owned it. And he never did buy it. He started talking about all that was wrong with it, dismissing the fact he'd been riding around in it for nearly half a year. I bought him a truck and he drove the other one over to the fella's house who owned it, got out and left it and ran back to my car and we drove out of there like thieves. But still I'm not seeing who this guy really is. He kept on complaining about all the bad breaks he'd had. How he had to live like a nigger. No offense to Leonard. That's how he put it. He complained about the shacks people let him live in, like maybe they should have fixed them up for him or moved him into their homes. These people weren't slumlords. They were helping the guy out because they felt sorry for him, and he wasn't paying a penny.

"He complained they wanted him to do work for his room and board. It was always somebody else's fault and always someone else's responsibility to get him out of his bullshit. The truck I got him wasn't good as he deserved. It had problems. He wanted better. He admitted he owed money for past hospital bills and to the IRS and said he couldn't work because they'd take what he made. I paid his bankruptcy off. And it wasn't a little bit of money. He supposedly took the money to a lawyer, but the bankruptcy never happened. I asked him about it, he got mad. Like it wasn't something I was party to at all. He came up with new excuses. All of them lame. I began to realize what I thought might be a spark of salvation down there inside of him, a sort of muted intelligence, was nothing more than stupidity and shallowness, self-centeredness and misplaced ego. He didn't really have any feelings outside of those for himself. He was a big con game. The level of his intelligence, if measured in inches, would have been just enough to get him up to where he could play in the toilet bowl with a long-handled spoon.

"I like to never got rid of him, and finally it turned ugly. I was prepared to call the police and have him removed. I dreamed fondly of my husband with his head on fire and thought maybe this guy would look good with a fire cap too. I began to think of them negative thoughts, you know. But I determined to avoid arson on another human body, not because he didn't deserve it, but because I thought I might not get off for it this time. I cut off his nookie. I cut off his food. I threatened the law. He finally got the hint. Besides, he knew it was all coming to an end. He'd been through it before. He had been working another sucker all along, some other person to feel sorry for him and to tell him how I mistreated him. So he went from my house to another shed. Last I heard was that person's hospitality played out and he went to yet another shed. Always living in sheds or garages or shacking up in someone's house on a cold night. Working all day long to keep from working.

"By now, if the sorry cocksucker had gotten a job at a filling station and put in all the effort working he put into not working, he'd be vice president of goddamn Exxon. Anyway, it taught me a lesson. There's folks out there down-and-out because of fate, but there's lots of folks out there down-and-out because they aren't worth squat. There really are bums, Hap. Not just homeless. And there's even little circus-sold fucks out there who are not down-and-out at all, but have plenty of money and work in whorehouses as pimps and strangle and kill and rob people, and yet they want you to feel sorry for them because they're short. I say, shit, riding dogs in a circus is good honest work compared to what he's become. Hell, fuckin' wood rats under a circus tent for spare change is even more honest work. You with me on all this?"

"I think I'm tracking," I said. "Except that part about the rats."

"Pretend I said chickens, or some kind of small furry animal other than a rat."

"Okay," I said. "I can visualize that."

We lay there for a while, looking at the ceiling. And finally Brett said, "Will you hold me, baby?"

I said, "Would you really kill Red he didn't show us to your daughter?"

"I'd like to. The urge would be there. But I guess not. Not just for that. But he doesn't need to know that."

"I guess I did. Does that make you feel bad toward me?"

"Nah," Brett said, rolling up close. "Sometimes I can be so mean I scare myself. And I got to tell you, he got me crooked enough, I could punch his ticket."

I took her in my arms. She kissed my ear. I turned and kissed her lips, our tongues explored. A moment later we were making love, and for a while I wasn't all that concerned about Red and his bloody head, his circus past, or even his torturous time in front of *America's Funniest Home Videos*.

16

Next morning we were tooling down Highway 87 on our way into Lubbock, traveling some of the bleakest ugliest goddamn terrain this side of the moon. It's the kind of landscape you think you'll fall off of. Every time we passed a scrubby tree—more of a bush really—I wanted to jump out of the car, hold on to the tree for dear life, lest I be sucked away into some sort of Lovecraftian cosmic vacuum.

Red, who Leonard had just quizzed for directions, was sitting in the back seat next to me eating his Hostess Twinkie breakfast. He said, with white filling on his lips, "I never claimed I knew exactly where The Farm was. I worked other locations when I was with the Bandito Supremes."

"This gets richer by the mile," I said.

Leonard said, "I suggest we kill him and just ask randomly at houses along the way where The Farm is. I think we got just as good a chance finding the place doing that as fuckin' around with this ding-a-ling."

"I think the three of you feel I ought to help you if I did know," said Red, "and I got to ask. Why should I?"

"Because we will kill you if you don't," Leonard said.

Red licked his fingers. "Well, that is some kind of incentive, I admit."

"We're gonna drive to the Mexican border," Leonard said, "and then, if you can't tell us where The Farm is, I'm going to shoot you. First in one foot, then the other. Then your hands and shoulders. I'm going to make it painful, squatty."

"There you go with the short slurs," Red said. "How would you like it if I called you a nigger, a jungle bunny, or a coon?"

"I wouldn't like it you called me honey, or even to a four-course dinner," Leonard said. "I just don't care for your sorry little ass."

"There's that little stuff again," Red said. He took off his hat and put it on the seat between us and shook his head sadly. The wad of bloody toilet paper was still stuck to the top of his head. He looked at me out of the corner of his eye, sadly, as if we were co-conspirators.

"Red," I said. "I don't want anything to happen to you. Really. But you got to cooperate. I'm not going to try and stop anyone from doing what they got to do to find this place. We want to find Tillie, and we mean to do just that, even if we have to try and read heavenly signs and directions in your steaming guts."

"Well," Red said, "I suppose if I don't do something to help myself I'll continue to spend my nights in chairs and eating Twinkies for breakfast."

"Absolutely," Brett said.

Red nodded. "Well, we need to see my brother."

"Your brother?" I said.

"Yep," Red said. "Herman. He knows where The Farm is."

"You said you knew," Leonard said.

"Sometimes I lie a little," Red said.

"What's with your brother?" I asked.

"He used to be a Bandito Supreme."

"If he used to be a Bandito Supreme," I said, "he may not cotton to telling us where they hole up. He might also con us a little, get us dead. You might con us a little yourself, Red. You just said you lied."

"I might lie now and then," Red said, "but I'm not lying right now. Herman is not only no longer with the Bandito Supremes, he's a preacher."

"I'm almost afraid to ask," Leonard said, "lest this story turn out to be as laborious as the Book of Mormon without the good parts, but how did your brother Herman go from being a Bandito Supreme to being a preacher?"

"I'm not sure that's such a big jump, from Nazi to preacher," Brett said.

"Very funny, lady," Red said. "You're one of those who has no respect for anything. Not even religion."

"Pardon me," Brett said, "I didn't know we were keeping you from prayer meetings."

"I don't claim to be a churchgoer, though I ought to be," Red said. "But I believe in the church, and I respect my brother for what he's doing. Witnessing to the lost souls of West Texas."

"I got a feeling anyone lives out here is lost," Brett said.

"It is ugly, isn't it?" Red said.

"I don't know why I'm persisting," Leonard said. "But I want to know about this brother of yours, long as it doesn't somehow lead back to that goddamn steak ranchero."

"Herman, unlike myself, is normal-sized. Well, that isn't

127

entirely accurate. He's large. Six four, weighs about two-forty, and can bench-press almost four hundred. Quite a bit of weight, I assure you, but as I explained last night, considering my size and weight and the fact I can bench-press two hundred pounds, he's not as strong as me, least not in a relative sense."

"Yeah," Brett said, "but how long is his dong?"

"I happily admit I have no idea," Red said. "We had very little boyhood together, and we spent none of it measuring each other's equipment. Are you interested in hearing about Herman, or not?"

"I said I was curious," Leonard said.

Red, feeling important, leaned back in his seat. "Any chance I might smoke my last cigar? I've been saving it, and since my incarceration by you three, I haven't had the privilege. From previous inspection I find that it's broken in two, so it'll be a short smoke."

"It'll be shorter than that," Brett said. "You aren't going to smoke it in this car. It'll make us all sick."

Red assumed a hangdog demeanor, but he was feeling too self-important not to continue his story. "Very well. As I was saying, Herman was normal, and I was not, and our parents deferred to him entirely. He could do all manner of sports activities well, while I, on the other hand, had a good mind. I could read and quote great passages of Shakespeare at a tender age. I hoped to impress my parents, but, alas, they weren't interested in a short Hamlet who they found embarrassing at public functions.

"At eleven years of age I ended up sold to a circus, apprenticed is the word they used, but undoubtedly, if you look at it clearly, it can only be determined that I was sold in the same manner you might sell a pup from a litter. It was purely a legality, this apprenticeship business. I was to be the circus owner's ward. The owner was a Mr.

Gonzolos. A nastier, fouler-mouthed, meaner-tempered man did not exist. He's long dead now. I heard from old cronies that after I left the circus an elephant—undoubtedly brutalized and mistreated like myself—mauled, stomped, and rolled on him. I say with only the smallest bit of shame, because he did keep me clothed and fed, I feel absolutely no remorse over his death. What I remember most about Gonzolos was that he constantly complained of hemorrhoids and lack of money."

"Unless the elephant is your brother Herman," Brett said, "I believe you've veered yet again."

"It's important that you understand my position in life to understand about my brother. He and my parents, in spite of their indulgence of him, had a falling out. It was about me, sad to say. Herman disliked the idea they sold his only sibling to a traveling-circus-cum-carnival-cum-sideshow, and they became estranged. Fact is, I have no idea what happened to either of my parents, and like with Mr. Gonzolos, I can't say I've pined over them much, and I'm sure there's no inheritance awaiting me. They never liked me, and they never had any money either.

"Herman fell in with some hooligans, spent time in jail, a bit of youth detention, and finally graduated to the big time. He got in with the Bandito Supremes, selling drugs. All of this he told me about, as I was not there to witness it. I was riding dogs and making a fool of myself in the circus at that time, but Herman went from being a football star in high school to selling heroin to twelve-year-olds. He did say that the bulk of his sales were to colored people, and at the time he felt that made everything all right. I can honestly say he doesn't feel that way now. He figures a colored person has just as much right to live and prosper as anyone. Herman has become quite progressive, actually."

"Yeah," Leonard said. "Speaking as one of those colored persons, I'd have to say Herman certainly sounds like a fuckin' peach."

"Would it be all right I merely suck on the cigar and not smoke it?" Red said.

"Go ahead," Brett said.

Red plucked the cigar from inside his coat. It was broken, but still together, held there by strands of tobacco. He pulled the cigar apart, returned one piece to his coat pocket, licked the end of the other, stuck it in his mouth and rolled it about as if tasting a Tootsie Roll Pop.

"I said Herman had a change of heart, became a preacher, and he did, but before that change of heart he put me on the road to commerce. An act he now regrets and that I'm most thankful for. Without Herman, at my age, I might no longer be riding a dog in the circus, but cleaning up dog droppings instead. At the time Herman removed me from the circus, my career was already in the toilet and I was heading in the direction of a flush. I had become surly, and perhaps it was my own fault that my career was eroding, but be that as it may, I was soon to be either working the dog pens or walking the street, giving blow jobs under the guise of a child prostitute, when Herman tracked me down by assistance of a private detective. When Herman arrived, I was more than willing to go in with him and start a new life and enter into his business."

"Selling drugs?" I asked.

"Herman started there, but he had graduated into a considerably broader program. Drugs. Women. Some money laundering. Getting rid of certain people. You name it and Herman was directing it or performing it. He located me at the circus, came and got me. There was a disturbance, a demand of money from Gonzolos. Herman refused.

'Hey Rube' was yelled, and Herman was forced to kick some butt.

"I had never seen anything like it. He was a human buzz-saw. I did my best, but being small, and having had little experience fighting, and being accustomed to losing all my fights, I doubt my contribution was of any significance other than to find myself tangled in Herman's feet. But he maintained his balance and survived the encounter by giving an astounding account of himself. Of course Herman was carrying a tire iron at the time, and this proved considerably to his advantage.

"Eventually everyone wore down and those with broken bones gave up gratefully. Even Bilbo the Strong Man, who I'm sure must have suffered a hernia after taking a full kick to the groin, not to mention a thumb in the eye, gave in and even cried a little. Size and strength certainly didn't intimidate Herman. As he told me later, no matter how big they grow, balls and eyes stay soft and a tire tool has no friends."

"Sounds like a motto to live by," I said.

Red nodded. "Herman took me with him, bought me my first tailored suit and got me laid. Also a first. There I was in my late twenties and I had never had the delights of a woman. She wasn't the best-looking whore. A fat lady with bad skin and an ill sense of fashion, but she was fairly quick-witted for a heavy drinker. She was a native of El Paso and for forty-five dollars she serviced me from head to foot. That is still one of my fondest life experiences, even if it did take place in El Paso and in the end she vomited on my knees."

"Spare the details," Brett said.

"It isn't my style to discuss sexual escapades, even if they were paid for. I was merely giving a general view. Herman put me to work for him. Oh, there were problems at first. My size caused some snickers among the Bandito Supremes, and Herman had to mess up a few people, but eventually I was accepted, and became good at the work. It was certainly better than riding a dog in the circus, and far better than shoveling droppings. It got so I could take care of myself quite well. Herman gave me some tips, see. And besides, as the old story goes, all men are created equal, but Samuel Colt makes some more equal. If one wants to be accurate, in my case it was Smith and Wesson that made me equal. I never cottoned to a Colt. Perhaps it's all that cowboy legacy. I hate that business. Can't even watch a Western on television."

"I think you protest too much about the cowboy stuff, shorty," Brett said. "Way you dress, you look like a regular Stick Horse Harry to me."

"There you go again, that demeaning manner. Television cowboys and fashion are quite different, lady, and I use that word loosely in your case. I'll have you know this is quite the fashion in some places."

"Yeah, some ranch on Mars," Brett said.

"So," Leonard prompted, "your brother took you in and trained you and . . ."

Red rolled the cigar to the other side of his mouth. "That's correct. Then, one day, after a long and particularly tedious job involving the nailing of a little girl's hand to a boat oar to show her father that business was meant involving some money he owed the Bandito Supremes for nose candy, Herman just cracked. I'm not sure why. He didn't do the actual nailing. He held her hand and I did that, but it did him in. He ceased to look at his work as business. He saw it as something personal. Always a mistake. You have to keep the two separate.

"He wandered off the job and disappeared for a year. No one could find him at first, but by the second year his

132

trail was picked up and certain Bandito Supremes were assigned to talk to Herman. It wasn't so much they were worried about his welfare, but he had taken money up front for the job, and though the mission had been completed, Herman had kept all the money to wander on. None of it went to headquarters so to speak, and not even I had been paid my share. It wasn't the money bothered them so much, it was fear of a trend. You know, Bandito Supremes bailing out on them and going on their own. Ignoring protocol.

"I was, of course, as you would suspect, willing to pass on my fee, but the big bosses were most unpleasant about it. I was able to slide out of working for the Bandito Supremes, and kept only a loose connection with them when I went to work for Big Jim. They were understanding. Herman having been my brother, they could understand why I might not want to continue with them, and honestly, they didn't care that much for midgets anyway. Eventually, I lost all track of them and their work except for when it crossed Big Jim's path.

"In Herman's case, they were less understanding. After he refused to pay them, they began to send hit men after him. Only problem for the Bandito Supremes was Herman was better than they were. He killed them all. I heard all of this through the grapevine, you understand. It got so it was a pride thing with the Bandito Supremes. They kept sending out these men to do Herman in, and he kept killing them, leaving a mark on them that could be identified as his signature."

"What kind of mark?" Leonard asked.

"It wasn't the best choice, but it was memorable. He took to cutting off the heads of their penises and putting them in their front right pants pocket. The police thought they had some kind of weird serial killer case. I read about it in the papers having no idea it was Herman at work. I suspected a mad Jewish rabbi. Later, as the story drifted back to me through old connections, I realized what it had been about. It was Herman's way of thumbing his nose at those who had been sent to kill him. A sort of manhood rite."

"Mine's bigger than yours?" I said.

"Exactly," Red said. "After three years of this, evading the cops and the Bandito Supremes, Herman began to seek out the Supremes directly, killing them on their own turf.

"Well, this would not do, but the Supremes had no luck killing Herman off. He was like a shadow. A ghost. A blood truce was made. People cutting their hands with knives and pressing them together like adolescents. Herman paid back the money and made an apology, and all was forgotten. As long as he never had anything to do with the Bandito Supremes again. This mean he couldn't even cross their territory without a threat of death hanging over his head. He agreed, got a job selling vacuums door-to-door, but never could move the super models, and that's where you made your money, so he dropped out of that, and next thing I knew he was a preacher. I've visited him several times, and he's tried to bring me into the fold. Though it's tempting, and Herman certainly gives a good fiery sermon, I find money and sex with average-size women more appealing than future paradise."

"You said average-size women," Brett said. "That mean you won't fuck a midget? That what you're sayin'? That sounds prejudicial to me. Not wanting to fuck a midget, and you being one your ownself."

Red refused to answer. He glared at her.

"This brother of yours?" I asked. "Where is he?"

"Southwest Texas. Near a little town called Seminole.

But I advise you to make your presence known gradually. Preacher or not, I doubt Herman would welcome a surprise introduction."

"We'll keep that in mind," Leonard said.

17

When we got to Seminole Leonard steered us through a drive-through, bought some hamburgers, then we cruised out of town to the west. It was a fair enough day, with cumulus clouds riding high and giving shade. Mesquite trees stubbed the ground all about, and behind barbed wire fences there were little patches of greenery mixed with prickly pear stands and dirt the color of dried peas. Sheep, goats, and windmills dotted the land, and the world seemed bleak and sad to me. All I could think of was getting back to East Texas. Back to greenery and creeks and rivers and the sky as seen through pine tree limbs.

After a while Red asked us to slow down, so that his memory might have time to work.

Finally, he said, "This is it. I remember now. This is it."

Leonard slowed, turned right, drove a great distance, came out on another highway, was directed by Red to the left, went along that way for some distance before Red said, "On the right."

On the right was a red windmill that had seen better days, but was still turning. There was a sign next to the road that read THE CHURCH OF THE BAPTISTS, and about an acre's distance behind the windmill in a clearing spotted with scrubby weeds was a little church made of plyboard, green lumber, ill-fitting windows, and hope. The church was warped due to the cheap lumber, and seemed as if it were about to pucker up and explode. The windows had cracks in the glass or no panes at all, and behind the glass I could see plyboard, and in one case some kind of thick yellow paper. The north end of the church touched the ground, while the south stood on dissolving concrete blocks, as if rearing up for a peek across the vast expanse of West Texas. The cross on the roof peak was weathered gray and starting to strip; it leaned a bit to starboard.

Out to the left was a wet-looking green slush hole that had to be the end result of a broken sewage line. Not far from that, like the husk of a great insect, lay an aluminum camper shell.

"Seems to have gone downhill," Red said.

We turned down a dirt drive. Dust rose around the car in white puffs thicker than the cumulus clouds above us. We parked out front of the church and got out.

Red was almost jovial. He coughed the dust away, started calling: "Herman! Herman Ames. It's me, Red."

After a moment the front door of the church moved, then caught, then burst open. A stout Mexican woman of about thirty came out and stood on the porch in a position that made me think of a wrestler about to get down and to it.

Red said, "Herman Ames. He here?"

She just stared at us.

"I don't think she speaks English," I said. "You got any Spanish, Brett?"

"Just rice, but it's back in the cabinet at home," she said.

"Herman," Red said again. "Herman."

The woman shook her head and moved into the yard, such as it was, ambled to the side of the church and pointed to the field out back.

" 'erman," she said, " 'erman."

"Gracias," I said.

The woman tugged on the swollen door again, pulled it free, disappeared inside the church. We walked around the side of the building and started into the field.

"Remember," Leonard said to Red, "I'd rather not poke a gun in your neck all the time, but you do anything fancy, or Herman thinks he's going to do anything fancy, I might have to shoot somebody and tell God he died."

Red grunted and we kept walking.

The field sloped gently downward, and on the other side, in the middle of it, we saw an elderly black pickup and next to it an apparatus perched on big wheels with thick transparent hoses attached to the main body. The thing, whatever it was, looked like a visiting Martian. The hoses were stuck in the ground, and a huge bearded man who had gone to fat was standing next to the odd device, watching us come.

"Is that him?" Brett asked.

"That's him," Red said. "Porked up a lot, but that's him," and before we knew it, he took off running.

The man by the apparatus recognized him, of course— aren't that many redheaded midgets around. Red ran right up to Herman and leaped. Herman caught him, lifted him above his head.

As we neared we could hear laughter, and Herman said, "Red, you old sonofagun."

"And you're an old sonofabitch," Red said. "Oh, forgot, Herman, you're a man of God now."

"The word couldn't be any worse than the sonofabitches themselves," Herman said, lowering Red to the ground.

Herman looked up as we came. He spent a little extra time looking at Brett. I didn't blame him. She was worth it. She wore a loose blue shirt and jeans tight enough you would have thought she had Levi legs. The wind had taken hold of her thick red hair, and the way it whipped around her head she looked like a goddess. Herman may have been a man of the cloth, but right then I don't think he was thinking about Bible verses, unless they were designed to give him strength.

Red said, "These are, I suppose you might say, associates of mine. It's a little complicated, actually."

"You in trouble, Red?" Herman asked.

"Kinda sorta," Red said.

Herman shook his head. "Well, let me finish up here, then we'll go up to the church and talk about it."

"What is this?" Brett asked, nodding at the apparatus.

"Well, lady," Herman said, "it sucks prairie dogs out of the ground."

"Any reason you're doing that?" Brett asked. "You don't stuff them, do you?"

"No. Ranchers around here hate 'em. Always digging holes for stock to get their legs into, and to keep them from shooting and poisoning the little boogers, someone came up with this device. I bought one, modified it to suit me. Church offerings weren't that good, so I needed a bit of a profession."

"Sucking prairie dogs out of the dirt is a profession?" Brett asked.

Herman grinned. "As a matter of fact, it is."

"Seems to me a device like that would cost more than it was worth," I said. "You aren't a rancher, are you?"

"No, but I got the dogs on my land."

"What you going to do with all them dogs when you get 'em?" Leonard asked.

"Sell 'em," Herman said.

"Who buys them?" Red said.

"Japanese are a big market. They pay up to five hundred dollars for the little suckers."

"Do they eat 'em?" Leonard asked.

"Oh, no," Herman said. "They make pets out of them."

"Hell," Leonard said, "for five hundred dollars them little suckers ought to clean your house and turn down the sheets."

"Just pets," Herman said. "There's Yankees do the same, only they pay about half that price."

"Well, I'll be damned," Leonard said. "Now I've heard of everything."

"Watch this," Herman said, and flipped a switch on the device. The motor whined, there was a sound like someone clearing their nose, and suddenly, riding up the transparent hoses, speeding along like bullets, came dark shapes.

"Wow!" Red said.

"Yeah," Herman said. "I think we got three of them that time."

"Christ," Brett said. "Don't that hurt them little dudes?"

"Just ruffles their hair, lady," Herman said. "And I doubt Our Savior enjoys his name being exploded like that for the sake of prairie dogs."

"Oh, I don't know," Brett said, "I was him I'd want to take a look at something like this."

Herman smiled, walked us around to the other side of the machine, showed us a transparent plastic cage where the dogs had been delivered. There were three all right, and they looked puzzled as all get out. I suppose I would too, I was sitting in my living room, was suddenly sucked up a hose and into a plastic container. I reckoned prairie dogs were developing a rather interesting set of stories about alien abduction.

"Well, ain't they the cutest little things," Brett said. "You don't just box 'em up and send them to Japan, do you? I mean, I can't see a bunch of them dogs in a box with air holes cut in the sides."

"I sell them to a distributor," Herman says. "He has them shipped. Big business, actually. After everyone gets their cut, I make about a hundred and fifty a dog. Most of the time. Sometimes the market's a little less."

"Looks to me like you'd run out of dogs," Leonard said.

Herman waved his hand expansively. "This is seven hundred acres, and it's all mine," Herman said. "Got it for a song."

I looked out over the land. Bleak and gray and ugly, with splotches of mesquite. I hoped he got it for a short song. A ditty maybe.

"Place is riddled with dogs," Herman said. "I farm 'em. I come out here and watch 'em some afternoons. Kind of educational, really, watching them pop out of their holes and look around. You get so you know when the babies are grown up enough to suck out of the ground. I don't like to get no little bitty dogs. I want them to grow up. Then I'll suck 'em up. If I was to run out of dogs here, there's plenty of ranchers be glad to see me coming with this baby."

Herman detached the cage from the vacuum and slid a perforated top over it. He sat it in the bed of the pickup. The dogs rose up and pressed against the plastic and pushed their noses to it.

The vacuum was hooked up to a little motorized device. Herman fired it up with a jerk of a cord, sort of steered it to the pickup by holding on to the back of it. At the pickup, he cut the motor back with a switch, pulled a wide piece of plyboard out of the bed of the pickup and fixed it so one end was in the truck and the other slanted to the ground. Pushing the throttle switch, steering the device with his hands, Herman guided it up the ramp and into the truck and killed the motor. He pushed the board up alongside it, said, "Y'all climb in somewhere."

Leonard got in front beside Herman, leaving me and Red and Brett to ride in the bed. We sat with our feet dangling over the open tailgate and Herman drove us slowly to the church, bouncing along the hard ground.

"I don't know why Leonard didn't let me sit up front with Herman," Red said.

"I do," I said. "We don't want you telling your brother a line of shit before we got time to lay things out."

"Don't think 'cause you're with some family," Brett said, "that everything is hokey-dokey. You're still our prisoner, and we still got guns under our shirts, and I'm just dyin' to hit you on the other side of your little punkin' head."

"There's that little stuff again," Red said. "There's just no peace from it."

18

The inside of the church lived down to expectations. It was ripe with the smell of sweat and boiling pinto beans and something baking. It was very hot inside, and Herman shoved at the swollen door until it hung open and a shaft of sunlight fell through it and hit the dirt floor and gave the cigarette butts there a sort of royal glow, as if they were floating in God's own butter.

There were four long pews to the left, and the closest one had a cot mattress on it with a sheet and a pillow that drooped over the side. The edge of the mattress, where it touched the ground, was brown with dirt. There were plastic cases with perforated tops in one corner behind the pews, stacked on top of one another, and in the cases were water pans and food pans and prairie dogs and newspaper lining and piles of prairie dog shit, both fresh and dry. The dogs reared up against their clear plastic cages and took note of us.

There was a wooden stove with a big iron pot on the top, boiling away, and the heavyset Mexican woman was stirring the contents of the pot with a long wooden spoon. She watched us with the same lack of enthusiasm she had showed us in the yard.

To the left of the stove was a doorway so narrow you'd have to turn sideways to go through it. The door itself was open, and I could see an ominous-looking shitter in there, stained black and green with a stack of newspapers by it, and on the other side a cardboard box.

Herman strolled over to the window with the yellow paper, pulled at the shade. It rolled up and light came in and made the place look worse.

Another step deeper and I could smell the prairie dogs and their offal, and it wasn't something that went with pinto beans and baked goods.

Red looked about, took off his hat and held it in his hand as if acknowledging the dead. "Kind of let the place go, haven't you, Herman?"

"Reckon so," Herman said. "People quit coming."

"You always gave a good sermon," Red said.

"Yeah, but I didn't give it so good in Spanish and most of the Mexicans around here are Catholics anyway."

"The woman?" Red said. "She a working girl?"

Herman laughed. "Girl. She hasn't been a girl since the Mexican Revolution. She works for me. Don't even know her name. She takes a hundred dollars a month. Comes in and cooks for me, and if she's in the mood, sweeps the place out. She'd service me for an additional fifty dollars a month, but I'm not interested."

"You still preach?" Red said.

"Just to myself," Herman said. "I hope I can convince you and your friends to stay for supper. Don't worry. She's

144

clean. The woman, I mean. And the food. The place could use some work."

"Perhaps a fire," Red said.

"Yeah, well," Herman said, sitting down on the edge of the pew with the mattress, "I call it home. How's about you tell me what your problem is, Red. You still doing . . . the work?"

"I was, up until the other day," Red said. "I was pulled out of it by this lady and these two gentlemen. They've kept me company these last few days, and let me tell you, it's been an experience."

Herman was looking at the wad of bloody toilet tissue on Red's head. "What happened to your noggin?" Herman asked.

"Oh, the lady here took a pistol to my skull," Red said. "And she made quite a time of it."

Herman stood up. Leonard said, "Sit down, Herman. You need to hear the whole story before we start hitting each other."

Brett pulled her pistol from under her shirt, said, "Hell, who's hittin'?"

"Everybody ease off and lighten up," I said.

Herman turned to the Mexican woman and said something quick in Spanish. She let go of the spoon, walked past us, right out the door without so much as a change of expression.

I said, "I hope you just told her to go to the house."

Herman nodded. "Go on, let's hear it."

"Red here says he's done some bad stuff and you got him into it," I said.

"True," Herman said. "I've abandoned that kind of life myself. I wish my brother would. If you're looking for me to give you connections, I can't."

145

"Nope," Leonard said. "We're looking for directions to The Farm."

Herman looked at Red. Red said, "Well, they said they'd kill me if I didn't show them where The Farm was, but I didn't know where it was, so I had to tell them about you."

"You're still involved with Big Jim?" Herman asked.

"I was," Red said. "These three may have queered me there." Red told Herman what had happened from when he and Wilber had put the bite on Brett for money, on up to the moment. I thought his telling was accurate, if overly long, and that goddamn steak ranchero came up again.

Herman sat with his head down for a long while, thinking. We let him think. I looked out the door and saw the Mexican woman trudging down the road, dragging little clouds of dust behind her heels.

"I don't know," Herman finally said. "This is some kind of situation. You've abused and humiliated my brother, and yet you ask me for help. You ask me to violate a trust, an agreement to never step foot on Bandito Supreme property again. I'd be tossing my life away."

"Directions will do," Leonard said. "You can stay here and suck prairie dogs out of holes."

"Yes, I suppose so," Herman said. "But then I'd be tossing your lives away."

"My suggestion," Red said, "is you let them toss their lives and just save mine. They hit me a lot, you know?"

"Yes, I see that," Herman said.

"It hurt," Red said. "They're capable of anything. I saw this one," he indicated Leonard, "shoot Moose's foot off. You remember Moose, don't you?"

"You do that?" Herman asked Leonard. "You shoot Moose's foot off?"

"Yep," Leonard said. "Thought it was kind of funny actually."

"See," Red said. "They have no conscience. You should have seen her pistol-whip me. I've never seen anyone happier."

"And I suppose you want me to do something about it," Herman said.

"It crossed my mind," Red said.

"In case you haven't noticed," Herman said, "the lady has a gun, and my guess is there are guns under the shirts of these two men, and you just finished telling me how ruthless they are."

"That's right," Leonard said. "And we're just full of whup ass too. And we got shotguns in the trunk, we need 'em."

"Lots of ammunition," I said.

"That don't do it," Leonard said, "we'll use rude language too."

Herman nodded, turned to Red. "We got a problem here, Red. First off, you're my brother. I love you. But you're a piece of shit. I used to be a piece of shit, and may still be one, but you are definitely still one."

"A matter of opinion," Red said. "But the words are particularly foul coming from the mouth of my own kin, and a man of God at that."

"They are neither foul or not foul," Herman said, "they're the truth. And I haven't been a man of God in some time now. There's also the fact I'm fat and not nearly as tough as I used to be. Or maybe I don't want to be tough anymore. Do you want me shot, Red?"

"Of course not," Red said.

"Then relax a little." Then to Brett: "This girl, this Tillie. She's your daughter? I understand that right?"

"That's right," Brett said. "And I want her back."

"She chose the life," Red said.

"She didn't choose to be taken to The Farm," Herman said. "You know what that means."

"I don't see how it's my problem," Red said.

"You wouldn't," Herman said. "I did you a great disservice, Red. Bringing you into the business. If I could undo it I would. You might have been better off with the circus."

"Don't say that," Red said.

"You're saying you'll help us?" Brett asked Herman.

"Maybe," Herman said. "I don't know."

"We could make you," Brett said.

"Maybe," Herman said. "Maybe you couldn't. Neither pain nor death scares me much these days."

"I might could show you a side of pain you haven't visited before," Leonard said.

Herman grinned at him. Leonard grinned back. It was great to see two sweet fellows bond.

"We don't want to make you do anything," I said. "We want to find Brett's daughter and bring her home. That's the end of it."

"For you, maybe," Herman said. "It wouldn't be for me."

"You keep talkin' like you got to really do somethin'," Leonard said. "All you need to do is give directions. We'll keep your brother just to make sure your memory's good. We find what we're looking for, we'll let him go and he won't even have to be involved in the ruckus."

"It's not that easy," Herman said. "It's not like I can give you highway numbers, simple landmarks." Herman paused for a moment. "Let's eat. Let's stay friendly. Let me think about it some."

"Eating's okay," Brett said, "but you got to think about it a lot. We can't let it drag into tomorrow. I don't know what kind of situation she's in. I don't know what's happening to her, or for that matter, what may have happened to her already."

Herman looked at the floor, then out the door. It wasn't the answer Brett wanted. I saw her swallow hard. She went outside and I followed her but gave her space. I leaned against the side of the church and watched Brett walk about in the yard as if she couldn't decide on a direction. I could see the Mexican woman too. She had really made some distance. She was down the road and to the highway. I watched her cross the highway, duck and crawl through a barbed wire fence, and walk out into a plowed field. She started across the field, dragging more dust clouds behind her. After a while I could only see the dust. It was as if the woman had disappeared into a cloud of sand.

Mexican ninjas.

Brett walked out to her car and leaned on the hood with both hands, as if trying to push it to the center of the earth. I saw her body tremble, her head shake.

I went over and put my arm around her shoulders and didn't say anything. After a time her hand came up and went behind my waist. She held me and began to sob.

Later, we had pinto beans and slightly burned cornbread and ate it off paper plates with plastic forks. We sat outside on Brett's car. This was much better than inside the church, except when the wind blew and picked up the smell of sewage or blew dust into our food.

I was watching Herman and Red carefully, lest Herman decide to break loose and try and shove Leonard, Brett, and me into a prairie dog hole. I was perhaps giving Herman too much attention, actually being prejudicial. Red was right. Something about him being small caused you to underestimate him. Maybe it was his way of talking.

Here was a man who had strangled a woman and nailed a little girl's hand to a boat paddle, and he consistently looked dazed and confused and about as dangerous as a wet newspaper.

I had to remember these guys weren't just a couple of goofballs, no matter how goofy they seemed.

We sat so that Herman was on the hood between me and Leonard, and Red sat on the trunk with Brett, who sat far enough from him to use the gun she kept in her lap. She was very nervous, anxious, and I was hoping Red didn't make a sudden dive to scratch his nuts or pick his nose, or he might end up with a .38 round in his teeth.

After a bit, Red finished his meal, slid off the trunk, and came around front. He said, "Do your facilities function, brother?"

"More or less," Herman said. "You got to flush it twice or three times, and if it overflows there's a plunger in there and a mop. Stinks some. It hasn't been cleaned in, oh, two years."

"Goodness," Red said.

"And you got to wipe on newspapers and throw them in a cardboard box."

"Maybe I'll just walk out in the field some," Red said, "do it down a prairie dog hole. I have some Kleenex in my suit pocket."

"No," I said. "Don't think so. I don't want you going that far."

Red looked at Herman. Herman shrugged.

"There wouldn't be a gun or anything in the house, would there?" Leonard asked.

"I disposed of them all long ago," Herman said.

"I hope so," Leonard said. "Don't go out the back, Red."

"There's no rear exit," Herman said.

150

"Then see you later," Leonard said to Red. "Happy bowel movements."

"Crude," Red said. "I'm the one being chastised here for my lifestyle, and the four of you are crude. Very crude. I can assure you, if one of us was invited to tea with the Queen of England, it wouldn't be you two or the woman, and I am sorry to say, it wouldn't be you either, brother."

Red went away then, trudging toward the church and the toilet, his head held high, his bowels contained.

"He's kind of prideful," Herman said.

"Hell," Leonard said. "He's just full of shit is all."

19

I suppose it was midnight. I hadn't looked at a clock in some time. I was sitting on the hood of Brett's car with my back against the windshield. I had my hands under my shirt, on my revolver, just in case I needed to blow Herman's brains out.

Above me was a great and beautiful canopy of stars. They seemed different stars from East Texas stars. They were brighter and closer. They looked sharp enough to cut your hand.

On the far side of the hood, stretched out, his feet dangling over the front of the car, was Herman. He had his hands behind his head and his eyes open. His belly heaved like a great turtle sleeping.

Leonard was in the front seat, stretched out, catching a catnap. Red was in the back seat. Red thought Leonard was awake watching him, so when Red went to sleep, Leonard took advantage of it. Brett was in the house, lying on the dirty mattress and the pew. She had spent two hours cleaning the prairie dog cages, feeding and watering the critters. Somewhere, buried inside her, was a housewife with an apron and fuzzy house slippers. Of course, in Brett's case, that internal woman wasn't wearing anything but the apron and slippers, and there was a shovel, lighter fluid, a box of matches, and a revolver nearby.

Herman spoke suddenly, "It's strange how a man perceives things. Once, I felt nothing. Then I felt everything. Now I feel nothing again, except remorse. I can't lose remorse."

"Not sure you should," I said.

"It's odd. I went my way and did the things I did, and one day I began to think about my brother. I hadn't missed him until that moment. Hadn't thought of him at all. I was like our parents. He was just an embarrassment. Then one day I'm in Dallas. I was there to kill a man because I had been hired to kill him. He was not an important man, but he had insulted a man who had the money to have him killed, and I was the man to do it. I had gotten the job through the Bandito Supremes. They are something, Hap. Once they were nothing more than a two-bit motorcycle gang, running a few drugs, selling whores. Now, they have little to do with motorcycles. They are a large clearinghouse for disaster, and they get a slice of every disastrous pie they bake. Part of that pie went to me. Anyway, I'm in Dallas and I'm not thinking about this guy I'm going to kill at all. I had already made up my mind how to do it and make it messy the way the client wanted it, and I'm waiting for nighttime when I'm going to do it, and I see these kids playing in the park, and one of them is little and ugly and redheaded and these other kids are picking on him. Hitting him. Tossing rocks. Yelling at him. Stuff like, 'We'd rather be dead than red on the head,' and the kid's running, and they're busting him from every side, and there's a kind of frenzy going on. I believe, down deep, in each of us, especially males, there's a hunter-killer switch of sorts, and sometimes odd things can set it off. We still have a pack mentality, and this kid was wounded, and the pack smelled blood, and they were all going for this kid, and though I can't say he would have died from it, he would certainly have been hurt. And it wasn't that I was particularly moved by children prior to this, but the redheaded kid pulled something inside of me, another kind of switch, and I could see my brother in this child's place, and suddenly I'm up screaming and I chased the boys off and helped the redheaded kid up. He ran away from me as fast as he could. That was it. End of story. But something moved inside me. It felt strange, and it felt good. Where the freezer had been, there was suddenly this wave of warmth, an open oven. I had never really felt that before. I didn't know exactly what it was. You know what I did, Hap?"

"No."

"I went ahead and killed my man. Then I went home to my parents. I hadn't seen them in years, and I shot them both with a twelve-gauge pump shotgun with remarkably smooth action. A Remington, to be exact, and if I were still in the business, it's a tool I would highly recommend."

I felt the hackles move on the back of my neck. I made sure I had a good hold on the revolver under my shirt.

"Very methodically I shot them, making sure they knew it was me doing it. I went down to Mexico and stayed there for a while, on The Farm, but the law never put anything together. The shotgun was cold. The crime was spur-of-the-moment. Nothing was taken and I moved on immediately. A fine method of operation I might suggest if you should ever suddenly decide to be a serial killer."

"Well, I am still trying to put a career together, so I'll keep that in mind."

"They were my parents, Hap. They were Red's parents, and they had sold him to the circus. Me, they had raised me with some kindness and respect, but I hated them. I knew when I saw that redheaded kid being chased and hurt that I hated them. It was because of Red that I hated them. They had sold him with no more hesitation than they might a pup from a litter, and they had gotten away with it. Somehow none of this had meant a thing to me before. Red had meant nothing to me, but that day I had a sort of epiphany. I sought Red out.

"It was quite easy to track him down. I went to the circus and bought Red back."

"I thought there was a fight."

"Red tells people that. I think it makes him feel less like a piece of meat to have someone fighting over him. Buying him back is only a little better than selling him. There was no fight. In fact, he could have left at any time. He just didn't have any place to go. I could have taken him away without money crossing palms, but I wanted to keep Gonzolos happy about the arrangement. I didn't want to draw any unnecessary attention to myself or Red. You've got to consider the business I was in."

"Red claims an elephant rolled over on the owner. Any truth to that?"

"I don't know. It could have happened. Red likes to put frills on his life. I don't blame him. It hasn't been a very special life. I took Red into business with me. He had the mind for it. He had been used for years, so now he was willing to use others. He was a natural, as I had been. Then one day, in Galveston, it became necessary to nail a young girl's hand to a boat paddle to make her father pay a debt, and in that moment, I had another feeling. I don't know how better to describe it. In the girl's eyes I saw myself mirrored, and somehow, where before I had been able to see people like paper cutouts, this time I could see this was a living, breathing child, and when she screamed it was more than a sound. Something snapped inside me.

"I just walked off. Went into hiding. The Bandito Supremes sent men after me. I killed them. Finally we reached a kind of peace. I got religion, but religion worked only for a short time. It allowed me to say, 'Yes, I have done these horrible things, but now I am saved in Christ, and I am a good man now, and I'm leading others to salvation.' Then, one night, like tonight, I looked up at the stars and knew in that moment there was nothing out there. Just like that it came to me. There's no God. There are just stars. And the stars are nothing more than dying lights, and between them is dead darkness. From time to time I still try and believe in God. I use his name. But now I know there's nothing there, and I can't hide behind God. I know who and what I am and it's very hard to face. And Red. He's like I used to be.

"It's strange really. Sometimes I look at a tree, or a bush, or whatever, and I see it for what it is. Something dying. Everything that lives is just something dying. It's not a wonderful revelation. I no longer feel the need to bathe or to even clean my surroundings. I want them as foul as I feel. Does that make sense to you?"

"I suppose," I said.

"I am bathed not in the blood of Christ, but in the darkness of lost revelations. A pompous way of saying there is nothing to my life but emptiness. Do you ever feel that way?"

"Sometimes," I said. "But it passes. As Leonard has

pointed out, I'm like the guy goes out in the yard and steps in a pile of horse shit, and where he or someone else would say, goddamn, I've stepped in horse shit, me, I'm looking for the pony."

Silence for a while. Then: "What I will do," Herman said, "is I'll take you to find this girl. I'll help you find her and take her away."

"Brett will appreciate that," I said.

"I will appreciate it myself," Herman said. "Perhaps I'm no less selfish than before. I'm not doing this for Brett. Or you. Or even to save my little brother. I'm doing it for me."

20

Next morning I rode with Herman in his truck to drop his prairie dogs at his distributor's ranch. Money changed hands, the dogs were unloaded, and we drove back.

When we got to the church and parked, we saw Brett out back of the place running a water hose over her naked body. In the rosy morning sunlight, her wet red hair cascading over her pale freckled shoulders, the thin line of fiery hair on her pubic mound, her breasts swaying as she bent beneath the water hose, I had a feeling I had just glimpsed what heaven must offer twenty-four hours a day. With maybe a fifteen-minute break for some kind of tonic.

With the water running hard, Brett hadn't noticed us. She swished, turned and bent and showed us her bottom, then turned and saw us. She frowned, shrugged her shoulders and went back to it.

We just sat in the truck, not knowing what to do. Finally, I opened the door and got out and Herman did the same. We walked around to the front of the church.

Herman said, "I just remembered why I like women."

"Yep," I said. "Me too."

"She's your woman, isn't she?"

"She's her own woman, but she lets me hang out with her."

"For the first time in a while, I want to take a bath."

"Just a few kinds words, Herman," I said. "You need it."

The door to the church was open, and when we looked in Red was tied up and gagged and lying where Brett had been. Herman went inside and began untying him. I didn't try to stop him.

When the gag was removed, Red began to sputter. "That nigger did this."

"Ixnay on the iggernay," I said. "I don't like it, and Leonard, he likes it less."

"He tied me up for talking too much," Red said. "He said I was a nuisance."

"You are a nuisance," Herman said.

"Et tu Brute?" Red said.

"Where is Leonard?" I asked.

"I don't care," Red said. "I can't believe this. He tied me up like a prize pig and left me here. He'll pay for that. My mother used to put me in the closet, lock me in when she wanted to be rid of me. I told myself I would never allow another person to do what she did."

"We've been doing it for days," I said.

"That's right," Red said, "you have. And I promise there will be reprisal."

"I'm going to help them," Herman said.

"What?" Red said.

Herman nodded. "That's right. I haven't done much

159

with my life, Red, and you've done nothing with yours. Let's do something constructive for a change."

"Rescuing a whore?" Red said. "Are we saving her from a fate worse than death? I have news for all you knights, Tillie's cherry has long been removed from the box and the cherry's consumed and the box is trampled, if you get my meaning."

"That has nothing to do with it," I said. "We're not rescuing her from sex. We're trying to rescue her from abuse."

"She's been abused so long she thinks it's foreplay," Red said.

"I think perhaps one day she figured out it wasn't," I said. "That's why she wants to come home."

Brett appeared in the doorway wrapped in a towel that didn't cover too much. Another towel was wound around her head and hair. She was carrying a bar of soap. "It's hard to have privacy here," she said.

"Wow!" Red said. "Lady, may I say you could be serious money on the hoof if you wanted to trade professions."

"No thanks," Brett said. "I borrowed some soap and some shampoo, Herman. My suggestion is you take advantage of it as well. And these towels could use some soap themselves."

"Herman and I were just discussing his body odor," I said.

"I hope you weren't discussing anything else," she said.

"Sorry about that," I said. "We had no idea what you were doing."

"And you spent a while making sure you had no idea," she said.

"We couldn't move," Herman said. "The blood had sunk to our lower extremities."

"I know where it sunk to," Brett said. "Leonard tied the

turd here up so I could shower and he could nap in the car."

"Herman is going to help find Tillie," I said.

"That right?" Brett said, and for the first time in days she looked excited.

"Yes," Herman said.

Brett walked over to the end of the pew where her clothes lay. She took hold of her panties, and very deftly put them on without losing the towel or giving us a sideshow.

"When do we start?" she asked.

"Today," Herman said. "The sooner the better."

Brett slipped on her jeans. It was like the reverse of a snake wiggling out of its skin. "That's good," she said. "That's real good." She turned, pulled the towel from her body, tossed it on a pew. With her naked back to us she pulled on her shirt while we held our breath. She removed the towel from her head, shook her hair, and when she turned the shirt was half buttoned and her hair fell against it and dampened her breasts. She pulled a long comb from her back pants pocket and began carefully dragging it through her wet hair.

"How long after you three get through looking at my titties are we going to do this thing?" Brett asked.

"We could look a long time," Red said.

"But we won't," Herman said. "We'll do this soon as the three of you are ready."

We talked briefly and made some general plans. Brett recovered her revolver where she had hidden it outside under an overturned bucket, stuffed it in her pants, and while Herman stripped off out back and bathed, we went out to see Leonard.

I opened the back seat door and tapped him on the leg.

He squirmed, and I tapped him again. When he rolled over, he had a pistol in his hand.

I said, "Howdy."

He put the gun away, mumbled something and sat up. He rubbed his neck and the back of his head and finally said, "First thing I want to do when I can is jack off, take a good shower, and sleep in a good bed. Maybe eat a steak and a bag of vanilla cookies. I need some cheering up."

"I don't feel so spiffy myself," I said.

"Me neither," Brett said.

"Sorry about that masturbation line," Leonard said.

"That's all right," Brett said. "I'd like a good fingering myself."

"Herman is going to help Brett find Tillie," I said.

Leonard nodded, got out of the car and leaned against it. He said, "That's good. I'm glad. When are we going?"

"Pretty quick," I said.

"Those two," Leonard said. "Can we trust them?"

"Herman, maybe," I said. "Red, not at all. There's other problems. We got to go to Mexico sneaky like. We can't just walk across the border with our guns and enough ammunition to start a revolution."

"Any idea how we'll do that?" Leonard asked.

"Herman claims he has a border connection," Brett said. "But it'll cost us some money. A thousand dollars. I got the money, so if Herman's telling the truth, that's done."

"I don't know," Leonard said. "I wouldn't trust either one of 'em far as I could throw 'em. Though, the midget I could probably toss pretty far."

"I hate that little shit," Brett said. "Far as I'm concerned, I'd put up a hoop and watch you make baskets with him."

"What's it going to be?" I said. "We going to trust Herman or not?"

"I have to," Brett said.

"No you don't," Leonard said. "We go Herman's way, but we don't trust him. We keep our eyes open and don't get too lax. I say we put Red in the trunk again."

"Suits me," Brett said.

"Not me," I said.

"Always the fuckin' humanitarian," Leonard said.

"He could get gassed, die on us."

"Your point?" Brett said.

"Amusing," I said. "But it could happen."

"He's right," Leonard said. "Then we got a dead midget to explain. Another point, we do this thing Herman wants, pay this guy to get us across the Mexican border with our weapons, what then? What about The Farm?"

"I asked him that," I said. "The Farm is a way station and pleasure house for the Bandito Supremes. Where they are, they feel pretty safe. Got authorities paid off, and there aren't any immediate authorities anyway."

"Recreation," Brett said. "That's what they're doing with Tillie. She's just meat for them. These Bandito Supremes want a little R and R, well, Tillie's there for them. Sort of like a piece of equipment in a rec room. It's disgusting."

"Way you got to look at it, Brett, is like this," Leonard said. "She ain't doin' nothin' she wasn't already doin'. She's doin' more of it and maybe in rougher circumstances, but it's not a new experience, so it's not necessarily a worse life than before. Important thing is, we're gonna go in there and get her."

"Herman says the place really isn't guarded that well," I said. "There's so many of them they don't worry much."

"How many?" Leonard asked.

"It can vary from time to time," I said. "Depends."

"So there could be fifty or a hundred?"

"It's possible. But there could be three."

"That's my man," Leonard said. "Still looking for that pony."

"Pony?" Brett said.

"Tell you later," I said.

"Anyway," Leonard said, "we're going to cross the border with all our little guns, then we're going to waltz in there and shoot the shit out of fifty, maybe a hundred guys. Or maybe three guys, and we're going to take Tillie with us, get back across the border, and head for the house. That doesn't sound like much of a plan, Hap."

"Herman thinks we can maybe do it at night," I said. "Go in and get Tillie and not cause too much of a ruckus. He knows the place well, and he knows the country around there fairly well."

"Here's the good part," Brett said. "Herman's connection, he hasn't seen in ten years. That doesn't work out, then we have to figure a way to get ourselves across the border."

"Then, if we managed to do this thing," I said, "we got to deal with the Bandito Supremes coming after us."

"I don't know that'll amount to much we get a good lead," Leonard said. "These guys are a bunch of thugs, not the Deerslayer. I doubt they could track sperm on their legs."

"Herman says the Bandito Supremes are vengeful," Brett said. "They'll follow us if they know who to follow. You'd think one little whore wouldn't be worth it."

"It's got nothing to do with that," I said. "It's that old macho mentality about crossing the line, and holding the line. Herman was lucky once. If they know it's him this time, they aren't going to make any pact. And besides, there's another reason Herman wants to go. He doesn't want to come back here even if they don't see him. He wants to start over. Sort of remake himself."

"He tell you that?" Leonard said.

"No," I said. "Not exactly, but that's what I get from him."

"He's got some kind of fantasy going he can take Red away from the life of a thug," Brett said, "turn him into something better."

"Yeah," Leonard said, "and a kind word to a crocodile will get you a smile."

"It all boils down to this," I said. "Do we still want to go in?"

"You know what I have to do," Brett said.

"Then you know what I have to do," I said.

"I don't have to do shit," Leonard said, "but since I got nothing but laundry waiting at home, let's do this thing."

21

We drove away from there just before noon, right after Herman set fire to the church. It caught quick and went up like oiled cardboard. Herman left a note and a hundred dollars on his truck seat next to the title for the vehicle. The note gave the title and the land to the Mexican woman. The hundred dollars was back wages. The prairie dog machine remained in the truck bed to go the way of fate. I wondered if the Mexican woman would take to it, start sucking dogs out of the ground to sell. My guess was it beat cooking beans and cornbread for a hundred dollars a month.

I was driving, Leonard was in back with Herman and Brett. Red was sitting up front with me, sullen and quiet for a change. I glanced in the rearview mirror and watched the church burn. For a moment, it looked as if it were wearing a flaming hat, then the whole thing was fire and falling lumber.

"So much for God's house," Herman said.

Man, this was something. An East Texas bouncer, a black queer, a ex–sweet potato queen, a six-foot-four overweight retired hit man and former reverend, and a redheaded midget with an attitude. The only thing we needed to top our wagon off were a couple of used-car salesmen, a monkey and an organ grinder.

Late in the day we reached the Mexican border. We stayed in a motel on the Texas side that night in a little town called Echo. Herman made a phone call to his friend, some guy named Bill Early Bird. I listened to the talk, trying to pick up on any code words that might mean bring about three hundred bad guys with shotguns and a lawn mower, but I didn't detect anything like that. Herman explained what we wanted in simple terms and hung up.

"We wait," Herman said.

Leonard decided to sit outside in the car with a shotgun, just in case the wrong crowd showed up. I loaded a shotgun myself, sat inside to the left of the door. Brett had her pistol and mine. Two Gun Mama. Red and Herman watched television.

About nine P.M. there was a knock on the door and I had Red open it up. Standing outside was a big, dark man who almost filled the doorway. He was dressed in a T-shirt, paint-splattered blue jeans jacket, blue jeans, and boots with paint splotches on them.

He looked down at Red, over at Herman, then around the door at me and Brett.

"Come in," I said.

He glanced at my shotgun, which I had moved slightly to the side so as not to look too unfriendly. He looked at Brett for a while. She held the handguns against the tops of her thighs like little lap warmers.

The big man came inside. Herman stood up and stuck out his hand. The big man took it. There didn't seem to be any great enthusiasm in the greeting on either part, just formality.

"Herman," he said. "How are things with the Lord?"

"Rocky," Herman said.

"I'm sorry to hear that."

The man had a kind of singsong quality to his voice. His face was pocked.

"This is Bill Early Bird," Herman said. "He and I used to run together."

"Long ago," Bill said.

Herman introduced me and Brett and said, "This is Red, my brother."

"Red," Bill said, and stuck out his hand. Red took it and Bill pumped the entire midget like a water pump handle.

Leonard appeared in the open doorway with his shotgun.

Herman said, "And this is Leonard."

Leonard shut the door, said, "Glad to meet you."

Bill nodded. "I take it, Herman, these men and this woman are not friends of yours."

"Not exactly," Herman said. "They are not friends of Red. I am caught in the middle. Please, sit down."

Bill started to sit, but Leonard said, "No hard feelings, my man, but I'd like you to come over here and put your hands on the wall."

Bill looked at Herman. Herman shrugged.

"I don't suppose while I have my hands on the wall you want me to lower my trousers, do you?" Bill said.

"Only if you want to," Leonard said.

Bill did as he was told. Leonard held the shotgun to the back of Bill's head with one hand while he patted him down with the other. Leonard removed a lock-blade knife from Bill's front pocket and a little revolver from a holster at the small of his back.

"You can sit down now," Leonard said. "Do that and we'll get along."

"We'll get along all right," Bill said. "All you got to do is treat me good and don't call me Chief."

"He doesn't like being called Chief," Herman said. "Bill here, he's a Kickapoo Indian."

"Long way from your original stomping grounds, aren't you?" Leonard said.

"What about you?" Bill said. "My people at least came from this continent."

"Actually," Leonard said, "my people come from East Texas."

"That might as well be another continent," Bill said, and sat on the bed.

"Story is you can get us across the border into Mexico," I said. "Carrying guns and ammo."

"Maybe," Bill said. "There's something I must get straight. I am not a great friend of Herman's. I know him. We have done some work together in the past. Smuggling. I want it understood up front that I'm my own man, and I've got my own help, and that's who I'm taking care of."

"Help?" Brett said.

"Two men," Bill said. "One is a pilot. The second man will help in other ways. I want five hundred dollars for each of us."

"Herman said a thousand," Brett said.

"Herman has no idea what I want," Bill said. "Prices change. And I don't do this much anymore. I have to make it worth my while. And frankly, that's pocket change."

"I can write you a check," Brett said.

Bill laughed.

"I can give you a thousand in cash," Brett said. "I thought I might need money for something like this. I have that much. A little more, but I'll need what's left for food and such."

"All right," Bill said. "You give me a thousand cash. Write me a check for five hundred, and put down on the check it's for car repairs. You get asked, I had to fix your brakes and balance your tires, do a tuneup. All kinds of things. You understand?"

Brett nodded.

"I have to talk to my men," Bill said. "I don't even know they'll do this. I didn't tell them anything. I wanted to see you first. I want to see some money now."

"You can see it," Leonard said, "but you aren't taking it with you."

Bill gave Leonard a strained look. "I have to advance my partners some."

"Why don't you advance them your best wishes," Leonard said. "They've worked with you before. Right? They trust you. Or do they?"

"Yeah, they trust me, but I don't trust any of you."

"But we're supposed to trust you?" Leonard said.

"I'm the man you asked to see," Bill said. "Not the other way around."

"This entire expedition from start to finish has been misguided," Red said to Leonard. "I suggest you let Herman and I go, cut your losses, and accept that Tillie is a whore and she is going to be busy at the quick-stop five-minute lube for the rest of her life. At least until she's too ugly to draw customers."

"I advise you to shut up," Brett said. "Or you'll draw flies."

"Another word out of you, Red," Leonard said, "and I'm going to see I can flush a midget down the crapper."

"Lay off," Herman said.

"I hope you don't think you scare me," Leonard said.

"I know I don't," Herman said. "But know this. The feeling works in reverse. You don't scare me. It won't be worth it for either of us."

"You people going to do business or what?" Bill said. "Personally, I don't care who's got the biggest dick here."

"Keep talking," I said.

"I say, five hundred now," Bill said, "five hundred when we actually start out, and you give me the check when we finish."

"Here's how it is, Bill," I said. "We give you two-fifty now. That'll keep you in paint thinner, but I advise you not use any until we finish up things."

Bill's eyes shifted away from mine.

"And I thought he was just messy," Brett said.

"There's paint all over his coat," I said. "He sniffs a little paint with thinner. They used to call it doing the bag. Sometimes it's glue instead of paint and thinner. But with Bill here, it's thinner. Am I right, Bill?"

"I'm not addicted," he said.

"I really don't give a shit," Leonard said. "You don't touch that shit until we're out of your life."

"Five hundred now," Bill said.

"We don't even know you'll follow through on things," I said. "Two-fifty now. Two-fifty when we get going. Rest of the cash and check when we finish the job."

"Things are hard," Bill said. "I need the money."

"Hell," Leonard said. "My thing is always hard, but you don't hear me whining about it."

"You don't know what life is like for me," Bill said.

"Oh shit, here we go," Leonard said. "Let me guess. You're displaced Kickapoos. Your culture is all lost. You don't get to hunt the sacred deer. You know what, that's

171

sad. Really. But, on the other hand, I don't give a shit. I'm fuckin' tired of the whining and the excuses for not getting on with life. I could sit here and give you my poor-little-nigger speech, but I won't. Because I don't see myself that way. My people came from a bunch of ignorant farmers, and so did Hap's, and he's white, and that's his drawback. Way I see it, I'm black and I'm human and I don't beg nobody for nothin'. So, you believe whatever you want, but it's not my problem."

"All right," Bill said. "I see where this is going. Take care of yourselves."

"We will," Leonard said. "Try not to track anything on the carpet on your way out."

Bill didn't move. He fumbled inside his jacket for cigarettes.

"Don't smoke that," Brett said.

Bill pushed the cigarette back into the pack. He just couldn't win. He hung his head. He sighed.

"Very well," he said. "I'll take the two-fifty now, and talk to my partners."

"I'll go with you while you talk to your partners," I said. "Then maybe you'll take two-fifty."

Bill didn't even try to argue this time. He merely nodded.

"You, Leonard," Bill said. "One word of caution. Watch yourself. Your mouth could easily write a check with me your ass can't cash."

Leonard grinned at him. "I can write a damn big check, Early Bird."

Brett opened her purse, peeled out two hundred and fifty dollars and gave it to me. I put it in my wallet. I took one of the handguns and put it in the holster I had clipped under my shirt. I said to Bill, "Can we find your friends now?"

Bill nodded.

"We'll keep your weapons here," Leonard said to Bill. "A word of warning. Hap there. He's one of those intellectuals, and he likes poor folks and puppy dogs, niggers, injuns, kikes and rednecks, white trash and midgets. He probably even cares you're a poor little Kickapoo done lost your culture. But you fuck with him, he will stomp your ass into next Sunday."

Bill looked at me. "That true, Hap?"

"Most likely," I said. "But just so you won't think I'm a complete humanitarian, I don't have any kind of thing for cats."

22

Bill Early Bird drove an old Ford pickup that looked as if it had been in a meteor shower. It had gray filler plastered all over it, and what wasn't filler was blue paint and not very good blue paint at that. Every time Bill stepped on the brakes the truck sounded as if it were in pain. The tires were so thin on tread you could almost see the air inside.

We drove through the little town of Echo, Texas, to the outskirts, crossed over a large overpass, went off the highway and down a dirt road and around a curve to where there was no real road, and still we drove. Eventually the overpass loomed above us, and beneath it I could see a fire, and when we parked and got out, I could see the fire came from an old fifty-five gallon drum. The air was cool and the flames leaped and crackled and most of the heat went up and away. There were some cardboard and plywood shacks under the overpass, and there were people to go with them. Four were visible, all Indians, squatting down, passing something between them, and as Bill came up and called out, two others drifted from the hovels and squatted with the others.

"Uncle," Bill called out to one of the men. "It's Billy."

An elderly man, built along the line of five coat hangers with two teeth and lots of gray hair, slurred back Bill's name.

Bill bent down and hugged the old man and the old man patted him on the back. When Bill stood up, he said, "This is my Uncle Brin."

Uncle Brin tried to stagger to his feet, but had to sit down. Not on his haunches this time, but on his ass.

"He's sniffed a little too much," Bill said. "Don't think he does this all the time. Just sometimes he gets down, you know."

From the looks of Uncle Brin, I had an idea that the only time he wasn't sniffing thinner and paint was when he was drinking liquor or was asleep.

Only one of the other men was elderly, or perhaps he just looked like hell. He had more meat on his bones than Uncle Brin, and his head was shaped oddly in front, a little like a pumpkin. The others were young and tough-looking, but wobbly. What the men out front had been passing between them was a paper sack containing a plastic bag containing paint and thinner. I saw Uncle Brin take the sack and put his face in it, and sniff.

I looked at Bill. He looked nervous, even ashamed.

Uncle Brin said, "Hey, Bill, go get us some smokes and some beer, huh?"

Bill nodded. "I will."

We walked back to the truck. I said, "It's nice to meet your relatives, but what's this got to do with anything?"

"Uncle Brin isn't a uncle by your standards. I suppose he is a cousin. But we call many male relatives uncle."

"Still, what's with him?"

"He's one of the men I want to use."

"No disrespect here, Bill, but he's skin and bones. What you going to use him for? A lock pick?"

"He's not always messed up."

Bill started up the truck and we drove off. Bill said, "He knows the other man I need. This other man, he won't do it for me. He might lose his pilot's license, but he'll do it for Uncle Brin. And some money."

"And Uncle Brin will do it for you for some money?"

"Uncle Brin will do it for me anyway, but he needs the money. This man who flies the plane, he owes Uncle Brin a favor for a favor done for his grandfather."

"Is it an old favor?"

"Yes, and one he has to continue to pay whenever Uncle Brin asks. He would do it without the money."

"He's that close to your uncle."

"They hate each other. This man, this pilot, he honors my uncle for what he has done, not for who he is or if he likes him."

We drove to the liquor store. I waited while Bill went inside and bought some cigarettes and beer. We drove back to the underpass and Bill carried the case of beer and the carton of cigarettes and set them down by the blazing fifty-five gallon drum. The men swarmed on the hot beer, opened it, drank it as it foamed. After a few sips, the carton of cigarettes was opened and packs were passed around and Bill produced a lighter and lit up one himself.

Bill turned to me. "I must talk to my uncle in private. We must speak in Kickapoo. Will you let me do that?"

"I suppose."

"I give my word I'm not trying to cheat you."

"I'll take it," I said, having no real choice. I went back to the truck, leaned against the front of it and watched to see if guns might come out. I also checked a good running route and something to hide behind. There didn't seem to be any good route, as there wasn't much vegetation or any real rises in the scenery. The best obstruction seemed to be the truck. I put my hand under my shirt and held the pistol butt and watched the men in the shimmering light of the fifty-five gallon drum.

Bill bent down next to Uncle Brin and they talked. Now and then Uncle Brin looked out at me and puffed his cigarette, each puff sucking his cheeks in, making them look as if they were touching inside his mouth. After a time I saw Uncle Brin nod. Bill hugged him, stood, and walked back to the pickup.

"He will talk to this man tomorrow," he said.

"You know the man yourself?"

"I do. But I told you, this man will not do it for me."

"You call him this man. Don't you know his name?"

"I do. But it doesn't matter. He will not do it for me if I know his name or not . . . Uncle Brin needs his money now."

"All right." I took the two hundred and fifty out of my wallet and gave it to Bill. He gave it to Uncle Brin and we drove back to the highway.

Bill and I made some plans and he dropped me off at the motel. Inside, Leonard turned off the TV, said, "Do we trust him?"

"I think so," I said. "Don't know we got a lot of choice if we didn't trust him."

I told everyone what had gone on. Herman said, "Bill

and I did some business now and then. He was never on the really bad side, like me."

"You were doing business," Red said. "That's all."

Herman ignored him. "Bill helped me run some guns and some grass. He helped me haul a few of the Bandito Supremes out of the U.S. and into Mexico. He arranged for an airplane. Some cars. He's trustworthy."

"He got paid, though, correct?" Red asked.

"He got paid," Herman said.

"That I can understand," Red said. "That makes Bill a professional. That's what's important. Professionalism."

"What kind of world is it where you got to do business with a crook?" Brett said.

"Kind where if you want to get something done illegal, you got to ask a crook," Leonard said. "Think about it, we're riding around with a crook and an ex-crook."

"I guess that makes us crooks," Brett said.

"I suppose it does," Leonard said.

"Seems to me," Red said, "I've served my purpose. If my brother is set on helping you, then he must, but I suggest you let me go."

"I don't think we want to deal with Big Jim right now," Leonard said. "We got a lot on our plate."

"Big Jim may not be all that interested in helping me," Red said. "In fact, I fear he thinks I was in on all this, and I would not be surprised if Wilber were not fostering that belief."

"How's that?" I said.

"Wilber has his good qualities, but loyalty isn't one of them. He likes money, and if he feels he can discredit me, put himself in the catbird seat, then he will. My guess he's making me responsible for all that business in Oklahoma City as well. Painting himself as a victim. That's my take."

"So if we cut you loose, where would you go?" I asked.

"I'm uncertain, but I would rather face that problem as it came to me than be with people who pistol-whip me, tie me up and humiliate me. I'm surprised I haven't been asked to perform some circus tricks. Some flips and handstands. Perhaps a cartwheel."

"Shit, that's not a bad idea," Leonard said.

Red gave Leonard a firm look, then slowly dropped his eyes. My guess was he feared Leonard might be serious, and that he would be forced to perform. Red picked up a can of Coke, swigged from it, then eased into sullen silence.

That night was not a good one. Herman was supposedly helping us. We didn't want to alienate him by tying him to a chair, and we felt it might be bad form to tie Red to one. Leonard and I, by unspoken plan, stayed awake with the shotgun. Herman and Red watched TV most of the night, dozing on the floor from time to time.

Brett slept all night on the bed and snored loudly. Who says it's a man's world?

23

Next morning Bill called and we made arrangements for him to come over before dark and lead us to our airplane ride. When he came we followed his pickup through town and out.

The town where we had slept, Echo, wasn't much. There were lots of tractors parked about and all kinds of yellow equipment that might have been designed for most anything. Farming. Tank warfare or prairie dog removal. In fact, Echo seemed little more than a town of old cars, old people, and huge yellow machines.

We drove out where there were no houses, no mobile homes, and no beauty, only long miles of dirt and brushy growth and soaring buzzards.

Miles later, we dipped down into an area between great hills and rocks and the falling shadows of the late afternoon. Beyond the hills, stretched out on a flat expanse of land that went for so many acres the eye could not follow, was a long tin shotgun building in front of which grew an oak that looked as if it might suddenly shed its sad sunburned leaves, keel over, and die. There was a relatively new blue pickup parked by the tree.

A man was sitting in a lawn chair under the oak, and when we pulled up close to the shed we saw he was drinking from a can of beer. There was a Styrofoam chest beside his chair. He looked to be a Kickapoo, or certainly to have a lot of Indian blood. He had on blue jeans, boots, and a leather jacket, which seemed inappropriate for the heat. His hair was oily and combed up high and flies had found it; they circled it, looking for a solid place to land.

Bill got out of his truck toting a pack of gear and four canteens strapped to the outside of it. We got out of the car, holding our guns. The man in the lawn chair didn't seemed surprised by any of it. He sipped his beer. Bill nodded at him, and the man nodded back.

When we were gathered around the chair, the man crushed the empty can, tossed it on the ground, pulled back the lid on the Styrofoam chest, clawed another beer out of the icy water, closed up the chest and said, "You got the money?"

"We got the money," I said.

He popped the tab on the can, drank from it, held out his free hand, palm up. I took two hundred and fifty out of my wallet and put it in his palm. He folded his fingers over it and the money disappeared inside his jacket faster than a teenager can stuff a fuck-zine into a sock drawer.

"We leave when it gets dark," he said.

"Since that might be an hour or so," Brett said, "why don't you quit suckin' them suds. I don't want a drunk flyin' me nowhere."

"You can stay here, lady," he said.

"Not hardly," Brett said. "I'm the one financin' this little shindig."

"I keep the money, and I drink the beer," the man said.

Leonard kicked the ice chest over, used his leg to sweep the chair out from under the man, who hit the ground, came up rolling, reaching inside his jacket. By then I was on him. I hit him with a backhand. It wasn't a hard strike across the jaw, but it wasn't gentle either. He went down on one knee and said, "Shit. I think you loosed a tooth."

"What the fuck you doin'?" Bill said to him. "They all got guns."

"I didn't mean nothing," the man said. "What's everybody so jumpy for?"

"Too much coffee," I said.

Leonard, who was carrying the shotgun, said, "You must have had one too many beers already, fuckin' with a bunch of folks got guns."

"I've had one beer," the man said.

"Must be one too many," Leonard said. "And it's rude not to offer us some. Everybody get a beer."

We did. We popped the tops and sucked on them. I didn't drink beer much anymore, but I enjoyed this one.

Leonard said, "And keep your hand out of your jacket, asshole, or you'll wake up with it in your ass."

The man smiled. "All right. All right. You're all tough guys. And one tough broad. Where'd you get the midget?"

"There they go again," Red said.

"We bought him off a souvenir rack," Leonard said. "But we lost the funny hat came with him."

"That's enough," Herman said.

"And you got a giant to go with him," the man said. He laughed and brushed the seat of his pants off, uprighted his chair, found a fresh beer on the ground and opened it.

"Where's the plane?" Brett said.

"In the hangar," the man said. "I'm not supposed to fly it. I'm not supposed to have it. I had my license taken away. I used to fly puddle jumpers for the U.S. Mail."

"And why did you have your license taken away?" I asked.

"I crashed one," he said. "Killed the motherfucker with me, which was no loss. I didn't like him anyway. I don't think that bothered them so much, but I lost a lot of mail. Burned up. 'Course, I kept some things and they found out, and I ended up nearly going to jail big-time. They didn't want the scandal, so I gave back the courier packet."

"What was in it?" Brett asked.

"Money," he said. "By the way. They call me Irvin."

The shotgun building was long and dark and hot. When Irvin hit the lights dust motes swam around like little sponges underwater and dust rose up from our feet in billows, and as our eyes adjusted we saw our ride. It looked like something you'd wind up with a rubber band and toss.

"Them wings glued on?" Leonard asked.

"It's better than it looks," Irvin said.

"I sure as hell hope so," Brett said. "When's the last time you flew it?"

"Not so long ago that you no longer recall how to fly, I presume?" Red said.

"Month ago," Irvin said. "But it's gassed and ready, and safe, long as you don't make too long a flight or get in too big a hurry."

"Or want to get airborne," Leonard said.

"It'll get up there," Irvin said. "It just heats up some you fly too long. Unfortunately, it's the engine heats, not the cabin. Not unless it catches on fire. Which, if we push too hard it could."

"Oh, that's good," Brett said.

"It's warm now, but come nightfall, up there, you best have some long jammies on under your clothes. It'll freeze your balls off. And in your case, lady, whatever's hangin'."

I turned to Bill. "This is it?"

Bill shrugged, "I didn't say I could offer you Air Force One."

"This is Negative One," Brett said.

When night came it turned cold as Irvin predicted. We helped push the plane out of the hangar, then boarded. It was crowded in there, us with our guns, and Red ended up sitting on the floor.

The plane's outside lights were dim, the inside control panel lights a sickly green. The motor sounded as if it would really rather not do this. The runway was bumpy. We left out of there with a bang and clatter and a sickening lurch.

We bobbed into the night sky and the engine coughed and sputtered and the propeller on the left wing stopped and started, eventually caught as it cast the remnants of a wasp nest away. Directly below us there was nothing but the dark land, and way to the left were lights, clean and clear and bright, like fallen stars. I assumed they were the lights of sleepy Echo.

We rose higher, but never really gained much altitude. The night grew darker, and Irvin was right, the plane was cold. It bit through our clothes and filled our socks and shoes and circled about us like a wraith.

Red said, "This is most unpleasant."

"Can we drop you somewhere?" Leonard said.

"Quite amusing," Red said.

"Yeah," Leonard said, "well I'd like to hear you laugh on the way down."

"Leave him alone," Herman said.

"All of you shut up," Irvin said. "Let me concentrate. Mexican Border Patrol, they spot us, they'll take a shot at us. Had a bullet come through this ole rotten floor once, ran up my trouser leg, come out through the skin on my knee. Close call. Didn't need any more than a Band-Aid. I got an iron plate under the seat here now, don't want to catch one in the balls or up the ass."

"How are the other seats fixed?" Leonard asked.

"Just cushions," Irvin said.

"Hell," I said to Leonard, "your balls are iron anyway, aren't they?"

"You know, you're right," Leonard said.

We continued to fly low, trying to stay under radar, if there was any, trying to take a straight line to where we were going, which, according to Herman and Bill, was on the edge of the Great Plateau and the Western Lands, some of the most inhospitable terrain in all of Mexico.

We flew for some time. How long I can't say. Couple hours at least. I nodded off to the hum of the motor, Brett and I falling together for warmth. When I awoke it was to a coughing engine.

"Is the engine playing out?" I said.

"No," Irvin said. "I'm lowering us. I make a change up, down, or sideways, the engine farts. I got to get some work done on it one of these days. Everybody grab your asses, we're going down."

Irvin cranked the plane into a steep turn, and down we went at an angle so tight we were temporarily lying on the side of the plane, then suddenly we were straight, being tossed about the cabin like jumping beans. Next thing we knew, the ground was coming up fast. I took hold of Brett and tried to remember my plan about going out between her legs, but there was no time for that.

The plane sputtered and spat and leveled out. We came in hot as a flaming hard-on, the nose down a little too much. At the last moment Irvin righted us and we smoothed out and the wheels hit and the plane hopped a few times and came to a jerky stop.

We got off, pronto. I bent over and lost what I had last eaten, which only reminded me I was hungry. Or maybe what I felt gnawing in my stomach was fear.

Leonard gave me some water from one of the canteens Bill had brought. I rinsed my mouth, then drank a sip. I looked around. There was nothing. Just a flat expanse of land, some rolling night-shadowed dirt, some brush clumps here and there.

Bill came over, said, "What you do is, you walk five miles that way." He was pointing to the west.

"Five miles?" Brett said. "Why the fuck not ten? Shit, you could have gotten closer."

"They'd have seen us come in," Irvin said. "May have already. I've run some stuff for them, and I don't want to lose jobs in the future. More than that, I don't want them to find me. I want to keep my balls, they give me ballast. You walk that five miles and you'll come to a place where there are lots of things growing. That means you are nearing water. Next you will come to an oasis. At the oasis is The Farm. You can't miss it."

"And if we walk five miles and there's nothing?" Leonard said. "We're in the middle of the desert and you've got our money, and come morning our asses are burnt crackers. I don't think I like this plan."

Herman and Red came over. Herman looked very big in the moonlight. Red seemed oddly smaller than ever.

"Bill's right," Herman said. "This is the area. We go in, we get the woman, we go out."

"You head southeast," Irvin said. "You meet the plane there."

"Seems to me it would still be easier to come back here," Leonard said.

"It would be easier, but it will be easier for them as well," Irvin said. "And like I said. They know this plane. I'm not putting myself or money I might make in the future on the line with these guys for your lousy money or your lousy asses. Though, lady, I must admit, you got an ass worth lining up for."

"That's enough of that," I said.

Irvin held up his hands. "Hey! Peace."

"This is rough country," Leonard said. "How we gonna know we're going the right way to meet you? What if they follow us? They're gonna see your plane then, aren't they?"

"They follow you that far then my ass is dead," Irvin said. "But truth is, you'll be lucky to make it that far. You'd be lucky to make it to the plane if I kept it where it's sitting. You'll be lucky you bring your asses out at all. I'm not sending you in there. You want to do it. It's your problem, and it's my rules for flying you back."

"Bill knows his way around?" Brett asked.

"Hey," Bill said, dropping one of the canteens and a small pack over my shoulder. "I'm not going. Me and Irvin will be waiting on you. I don't owe you a fuckin' thing. We'll give you till tomorrow night, late, then we fly back to Texas. You don't show up, may I now extend my best hopes and wishes that it all ends quickly."

"I know the country," Herman said. "I can lead you through it. I know where Irvin wants us to meet. It's maybe ten miles on foot."

"Ten miles!" Leonard said. "I say the goddamn plane waits for us here."

"If you can find transportation, take it," Bill said. "You people have a change of heart, I'll take you back. Now. But no refunds."

"I just want to get Tillie," Brett said.

"That's what we do, then," I said.

"Red stays with the plane," Herman said.

"Capital idea," Red said.

I looked at Leonard and he shrugged.

I looked at Brett. "Whatever," she said.

"Good," Irvin said. "It's decided. Good luck and all that."

Bill said, "There's some food in the pack, some blankets to put around you if you get cold. A knife. Matches. Some odds and ends. Light stuff. Don't worry about returning it."

Bill and Irvin started back to the plane.

Red said, "Take care of yourself, Herman. If it is you or these people, make it you. I think you and I can start our own business when you come out of this. To hell with Big Jim. We both have the experience. What do you say?"

"I say we talk later," Herman said.

Red shook hands, hugged his brother, and went back to the plane.

Herman pulled the pack off my shoulder. "We'll take turns with this."

Herman started out across the wasteland.

We followed, carrying our guns.

24

We hadn't gone very far when we heard the plane lift off. We looked back and saw it make a half circle and head south, a great shadow against the night sky, a couple of weak red lights burning.

"We won't see them again, will we?" Brett said.

"Probably not," I said. "We just got to do this as best we can."

"Bill will make Irvin wait the allotted time," Herman said.

"Your brother?" Leonard asked. "He going to make him wait?"

"Red . . . I can't say," Herman said. "Red has feelings for me when I'm present, but I suspicion out of sight out of mind to some extent."

We walked for a long time, eventually began to notice there was more foliage. It was sparse at first, like a few pimples on a teenager's face, then it became thick as acne, dark and full in the moonlight. Finally there were scrubby trees. We came to a slight rise, and just before topping it, I took the pack and canteen from Leonard, who had been carrying it, and we all shared water. Satisfied, we started over the rise and stopped suddenly.

Down below in a place not deep enough to be a valley, but lower than the land we had crossed, there was a very green expanse and there was a log cabin built ranch style. The logs had obviously been hauled in. There wasn't a tree anywhere big enough to hollow out into a canoe, let alone build a house.

The cabin was brightly lit and there was a lot of activity inside. We could hear someone singing. Badly. And there was laughter and loud talk.

Off to the right of the cabin was a great pool of water and in the middle of the pool was a huge water pump under an open shed. There was a bridge that ran from the shed to the cabin. The water looked like ink in the moonlight. To the left of the cabin was a corral, and in it were horses and mules; the mules easily distinguished by their tall ears.

Further left was a huge tank, heating fuel most likely, and beyond that a satellite dish, and further left a barn like you would expect to find somewhere in Iowa. There were two jeeps parked out front.

To prevent being outlined in the moonlight, we all hit the dirt and lay on top of the rise. Leonard said, "This has to be it."

"This is it," Herman said. "I've been here. I came by plane and was driven in by jeep by a slightly different route. I remember it well. It's kind of a country club, if what you like to do instead of golf is drink, pill, and screw. You'd be amazed how well equipped it is. Television. Movies. Horseback riding."

"We put one of the vehicles out of commission, take the other," Leonard said.

"What we do first," Herman said, "is slide down there and see what's happening. Try and locate Tillie. There's a chance she might not even be here. If she isn't, we slide right on back, head to the plane on foot, and they never know we've been here."

"He has a point," I said.

"I'll snoop down there, see if I can locate Tillie," Leonard said. "I see her, I'll come back and report. Then you disable one of the rides, Herman, hot-wire the other. Being a former career criminal, I assume you know how to do that."

"I can manage," Herman said.

"Then it's you and me, Hap," Leonard said. "We go down there and open up a can of blazing whup ass with a lava chaser."

"You and Hap and me," Brett said.

"If you insist on being modern," Leonard said. "Me and Hap and you. One thing though, I go down there and you hear gunfire, don't think I want to do the noble thing. You know, like have you leave my ass so you can escape. You come down there with guns blazing."

"They'll think it's the Battle of the Bulge," I said.

"I'll take the honky spreader," Leonard said.

I had been carrying it. I traded it for the standard pump shotgun. Brett was carrying one of the modified Winchesters. We had given Herman the other one. With some reluctance I gave him ammunition to put in it. I gave Leonard shotgun shells, fixed me and Brett up with loads.

"I'm so goddamn scared I'm shaking," I said.

"I get scared," Leonard said, "my dick gets hard."

Leonard slipped the strap of the shotgun over his shoulder, went quietly and quickly over the rise on his stomach and began to crawl toward the ranch house.

Herman said, "I hope he knows what he's doing."

"Trust me," I said. "He did this in Vietnam. He's got a houseful of medals to prove it. He's forgot more about stalking than you and me and Natty Bumppo ever knew."

"Yeah, well," Herman said, "let's hope the stuff he's forgotten isn't the important stuff."

The ground was pretty flat, but the brush grew thick now and was full of shadow. Leonard used this as his protection, crawling close to the ground.

I was starting to get giddy. Perhaps I needed a nap. A long vacation. Maybe Tillie was better off where she was and I was better off back at the house with Brett. I began to hanker for my bouncing job. I began to view working in the rose fields as a good time. I tried not to think too much about what I was doing. I didn't want to shoot anybody, but I didn't want to get Brett, Leonard, or myself killed by not shooting anyone.

I tried not to think about it. Trying not to think about it turned out to be a lot like thinking about it. I looked at Brett. She was peeking over the rise, watching Leonard slither down there. The moonlight fell across her face, and normally moonlight softened it, but now, without makeup, it looked hard and harsh, almost corpse pale. Her eyes were narrowed and her mouth, normally full and inviting, was a thin line. Her hair was bound back severely with a black ribbon. She held the Winchester like someone who wanted to use it and might be disappointed if she didn't get to.

I thought she was the most beautiful woman I had ever seen.

"He's up to the house," Herman said.

"Someone comes out of the house, points him out, we got to start shooting right then," I said. "Maybe we should trade guns, Brett. Modesty aside, I can shoot the ass off a fly at a hundred yards."

"I'm a good shot myself," Brett said.

"Yeah, but I'm going to venture I'm better," I said. "Leonard says I'm the best there is."

"Like he knows everything," Brett said.

"Don't let him hear you say I said it, but about some things he knows more than anyone has a right to. Like how well I shoot. You get inside, maybe you should have the shotgun. Easy to handle, spreads people all over the place. It's alternately loaded with buckshot and slugs."

Brett thought a moment, traded weapons with me.

"You start getting heated up," Herman said to Brett, "mind where you're firing that thing."

I eased up slightly on the rise, lay the dark-barreled Winchester on the dirt mound, and pointed it down there. I saw a man come outside lighting a cigarette. Behind him, through the open door, came the sound of music and laughing. I saw a woman in a red dress walk by. She was long and lean with big breasts and reddish hair. I couldn't see her face.

Tillie?

I drew a bead on the man. He closed the door, clung close to the wall, finally fell away from it, staggered into the foliage, shook his head, slapped the back of his neck as if to wake himself. He opened his fly and started pissing while he smoked.

A shadow came off the ground and fell down on him and the cigarette shot out of the man's mouth and the man went down. A moment later he was dragged into the foliage.

"Leonard must have knifed him," Herman said.

"Strangled him," I said. "Leonard can constrict those arteries, crush your windpipe while you're still trying to decide what's happening. That's one down."

"But the question is," Brett said, "one of how many?"

"I don't think there's a lot," Herman said. "You can't judge by the transportation, 'cause a lot of people get dropped off here. They hang out two or three days, then back to work. Kind of like a company picnic. Except for the whores. A lot of them get on the wrong side of these guys while they're drinking and boozing. Throw in sex and the fact these people don't have to pay for anything they do . . . Bad combination."

"These people?" Brett said.

"Yeah," Herman said. "I was one of them. But not now."

I saw Leonard move out of the brush and over to a window, then away from it. He peeked in another, went around the side of the house and past the corral. The horses and mules rumbled about, then he was behind the house and out of sight.

We waited and watched a long time.

No Leonard.

I was beginning to get worried when I heard him speak softly behind us. "It's me," he said. "Don't anybody shoot."

"Goddamn, Leonard!" Brett said. "I damn near threw a turd."

"Sorry," Leonard said, squatting on the ground.

"You're good," Herman said.

"Yeah," Leonard said. "I know."

"What's it like?" I said.

"Bad," Leonard said. "In the front room I counted ten. It's a big house. I went all around it. The windows at the back are covered. I could hear activity in the back room. Sex."

"Did you see Tillie?" Brett asked.

"I think so," Leonard said. "I saw three women. There's one looks something like Tillie's picture, but I think maybe she's had some work done."

"Work?" Brett said.

"I think she . . . or they . . . had her lips filled with collagen, or whatever that stuff is makes women look like they just got punched in the mouth. She's got red hair. A red dress on."

"I saw her pass the doorway," I said.

Leonard nodded. "I think maybe she's had something done to her nose and cheeks too. Sort of Barbie-dolled up. But I'm pretty sure it's her."

"Maybe we wait awhile till everyone's good and drunk or drugged," I said.

"You never know when a new group comes in," Herman said. "The girls down there, they don't get much rest. Truth is, they keep 'em so hyped on pills, they lose a lot of 'em. They keep 'em fired up because the traffic is constant. But one of 'em keels over, there's plenty of sand to put them under out there, and there's always a new one to bring in."

"I don't need to hear any more," Brett said.

"I take the front," I said. "Leonard, you take the back. I assume there's a back door?"

"Yeah, but the hot action is up front," Leonard said. "You and me ought to go in together. It'll take both of us. We maybe can surprise them and take Tillie out without having to get too active. In the meantime, Herman has to put one of the vehicles out of whack, and hot-wire the other. Unless you can do that, Brett."

Brett shook her head.

"Then you got to go in the back, Brett," Leonard said. "You got to go in there meaner than a junkyard dog with a hot poker up its ass. What you see that ain't Tillie, ain't one of the working girls, you may have to shoot."

"And you have to watch the working girls," Herman said. "They have odd loyalties sometimes."

"You got to grab Tillie if you see her and take her out whichever way is out," Leonard said. "You got to try and grab the ride Herman's wiring. And Herman, you got to protect that ride and cover our asses when we come out."

"Done," Herman said. "I'll go down now. When I wave, one jeep's dead and the other is hot-wired. Get the woman, and we're out of here."

"When Herman waves," I said, "you go first, Brett. Go wide and around back. You don't enter. You don't do shit until you hear us up front. When we let loose, you count to three. Slowly. Then you go in the back. If it's locked, blow off the lock and kick your way in. Remember, when you crank down on that baby the first shot will cover half the room. The second, the slug, will knock a hole in someone about the size of your fist."

Leonard gave Herman his lock-blade knife.

"Luck to us all," Herman said, and he went over the rise and down.

25

Herman made it, poked a knife in the tire. We could hear the air go out of it all the way up the hill. But no one came out of the house. The music was loud and no one was on guard. It wasn't a place they thought they had to be on guard.

Herman cut the rest of the tires. We could hear the air from them as well. Herman waved at us. Brett took a deep breath. I said, "Remember, it gets down to brass tacks, hon, you cover your ass."

"I will," she said, and kissed me.

"Go wide," Leonard said. "No hurry. Take it easy. We'll watch till you get behind the house before we make a move. Find some place to lay down back there and wait for our noise. When you hear it, let it be a starting gun. Don't think about it. You come through that back door like you're ten feet tall and bulletproof."

"I think I can do this," Brett said.

"You can't," I said, "just hold your position out there somewhere. We'll do what we can."

"I can do it," Brett said. She turned and ran wide along the low ridge, went over it stooping, making a wide circle toward the back of the house.

Leonard rolled over on his back and stuck out his hand and I shook it. He said, "Good luck, brother."

"Ditto," I said.

"When this is over, Hap, what you say we make something of our lives?"

"I'd like that."

"I mean it this time."

"I mean it every time."

"But it don't change."

"I mean for it to."

"We got to do more than mean it this time. It's got to happen."

"Maybe I don't know how to change."

"We're going to learn how. Got me?"

I saw that Brett had gone wide and was now behind the house. Herman was out of sight. Most likely in the jeep. I said, "Watch your ass, Leonard."

"You too," he said, and grinned at me. The moonlight made his teeth seem magnificently white, as if they were lit by blacklight. I gave him a pat on the arm and we eased over the rise on our bellies, made a Y. Me to the left, Leonard to the right. We were about thirty feet apart, crawling toward the thick clusters of brush in front of the house. It was slow go and hard on the body, especially since I was toting a few more pounds than I needed. The air seemed clean and sharp as a knife inside my lungs. My mouth was dry. My body seemed disconnected from my mind. As if I were standing up on the hill watching myself ease down toward the house. I tried not to think beyond the moment. The moment was all that mattered now. I had to be alert. I had to be ready.

Quit thinking about the moment, goddammit, about being ready. Just be ready. Keep crawling. An inch at a time. Eyes open, ears alert. Reach down inside yourself and find that primal part of yourself. The old reptilian brain. The part of the mind that is nothing more than motor response; the part that's pure survival. Don't think, just do.

The brush was sharp with thorns and bristles and it tore at my light jacket. I slipped out of the jacket, took the Winchester shells from it, and put them in my right back pocket. I took the pistol out of the jacket and slipped it in my left back pocket. I crawled on.

A sidewinder rattlesnake slithered in front of me and went into the brush. It was all I could do not to leap up and start running. All I could do not to open fire on it.

I thought, you're going to run like hell from a snake, but you think you're going to kick open the front door of a house full of bad-asses and go in there shooting?

Reptilian brain, my ass.

You are one crazy sonofabitch, Hap Collins.

Finally I bellied within twenty feet of the cabin. Around the door the vegetation was cleared. I could smell food coming from under the crack of the door. Steak maybe. My stomach rolled over. It was loud and rambunctious in there. They were playing ZZ Top's "Legs." Just a bunch of guys having a party. Drinking and doping and dancing and banging whores. Who was I to interrupt them? I didn't make Tillie a whore. I didn't ask her to run with the wrong crowd. I didn't even know her.

I turned my head. I couldn't see Leonard, just brush. After a moment he raised his hand above the brush. We both rose and darted toward the door. I stopped on the left side of the entryway, Leonard on the right. He looked at me. I took a deep breath and nodded.

Leonard turned the knob, swung the door open, stepped in and I went in behind him. He fanned right, I fanned left. At a glance I saw eight men. One of them, a black man, was lying on the floor in a pool of blood. Another black man was sitting in a chair beside him holding the dead man's head, saying over and over, "That nigger's dead. I killed that nigger."

As everyone turned to look at us, the black man kept repeating himself. "That nigger's dead. I killed that nigger." Apparently he and his buddy had had an altercation, and now his buddy was gradually assuming room temperature. No one else seemed in the least bothered by this.

There were two women in the room, and one of them, a pretty black girl, naked except for a T-shirt that almost covered her breasts and none of her bottom, wobbled over to the wall, stepped in the dead man's blood and sat her naked ass in it. "Wow," she said. The other woman, whose hair was so bleached it looked like cotton candy, was completely naked and being held up by a man so small his head was just under her left breast. As she wobbled, his greasy hair kept lifting it as if it might be trying to wave.

"Who the fuck are you?" said one of the men. He wore leather pants and work boots and was shirtless. He was balding and bearded and had a big belly. Tattooed on his belly was a blue and red eagle with a stick of lit dynamite clutched in its beak. On his chest was tattooed I LICK PUSSY LIKE A DOG. In green letters. Very festive. I didn't worry about what was tattooed on the knuckles of both hands. Too far away. But I figured it was easily on the intellectual level of the chest tattoo.

"Everybody shut up," I yelled over the music. "We're here for Tillie."

"Tillie?" said another man. "Who the fuck's Tillie?"

"It got to be one of the whores," said the black man.

"Man, y'all ain't none of us?" said another.

"No shit," Leonard said. "All you got to do is give us Tillie, and we will be on our way."

"You can get right back to cutting one another, fuckin', and dancing," I said. "Just as soon as we take Tillie out that door. By the way, you need to bury that motherfucker on the floor. That stuff running out of him isn't prune juice."

The guy with the tit on his head said to the woman he was holding up, "You Tillie?"

The stoned woman shook her head. "I don't think so."

That was when one of the men in the back, either less stoned than the others or more so, produced a handgun quick as a bunny fucks and fired it. The shot hit me in the shoulder, and without really knowing how, I was on the floor. Then I heard Leonard cut down with the shotgun and the middle of the room went away. Lick Pussy Man had a hole in his eagle and a couple guys were lying on the floor in his blood, moaning. The gun roared again and the guy with the handgun spun around and landed face first. What was left of his head flowed across the floor.

Time stood still. I got hold of the Winchester and used it to help myself up. Now I felt pain. There was a roar at the back of the place, followed by a yell, then another roar. The door at the rear flew open and there was Brett, followed by the stench of gunpowder. A wreath of smoke circled around her head, blood was sprinkled on her face, blood was on the wall behind her. One hand was clamped on Tillie's elbow, the other held the shotgun pushed up against her hip. Tillie was zonked and completely naked. Like her mother she was a real redhead. Leonard had been right, there had been some work done on her face, but it was her.

"Out of the way!" Brett said. "Fuck out of the way. I'll shoot any fucker in my way."

Those still standing parted. Brett and Tillie went between us and out the door. Brett's face looked demonic. Tillie looked as if she might be trying to add up a hard math problem.

A couple of men, half dressed, but holding heat, rushed out of the back room. A woman peeked out between them, then turned and went away. The men were in the room now, both zonked as lords, but trying to sober. "What the fuck?" one of them said. "What the fuck?"

"Avon," Leonard said. "And we mean business."

Then I suppose it all came together for everyone, what was really happening. Pistols snapped out of back pockets and ankle holsters. I cut down the Winchester, cocking and firing. Metal bees buzzed by me, and I kept firing. People seemed to leap away from me, and I saw the girl who had been using her tit for a hat go back in a blaze of flesh and bone as one of my wild shots hit her in the chest. I pivoted to look at the woman sitting on the floor. She was pulling a pistol out from under the dead black man's shirt and pointing it at me. I turned and fired and the shot drove her head back into the wall and the other black man yelled something at me and I saw he had a gun and I fired. I had gone prehistoric, sniffing that swamp gas and tar. I think I shot him three times. All I know was a moment later I was cocking and pulling the trigger on an empty rifle. I heard Leonard letting fly again, realized he'd been blasting all the time, then through the back door, out of other rooms more men began to pour. They had shotguns and pistols and no sense of personal safety.

I cut down with the shotgun barrel and it was as if a great and invisible wave tore through the fresh recruits, then I was yelling to Leonard to back out of there, and out he went, and me after him, the wall splintering behind us, the men from the back rooms falling over the bodies of their comrades, slipping in their blood.

I said we backed out of there. Hell, we ran out of there. The jeep came whipping up to the door. We jumped in and Herman lifted his rifle with one hand and fired at the doorway, then he dropped it, grabbed the steering wheel, and away we went.

Just as I was easing myself to a sitting position, there was a blast and I felt stings all over my lower left side. Leonard cut down on those behind us and Herman stabbed the accelerator through the floor. We bolted up and over the ridge where we had hidden earlier, and turned south. Behind us more bullets popped and hissed, but now we were running on the other side of the ridge and they couldn't see us and their shots were striking the dirt.

"Holy shit!" Brett said. "Holy fucking shit!"

"Shit," I said. "We killed a bunch of people, Leonard. We killed a bunch of people."

"Of course we did," Leonard said, putting a hand on my shoulder, pulling it back as he felt the blood. "Of course we did."

"Oh, God," Brett said. "They weren't so tough, were they? Were they?"

My thigh began to ache. I looked down. It was bleeding, turning my pants wet. My side hurt. I reached over and felt it. Small wounds. Pellets under the skin. I felt limp.

Behind us I saw a blur of white. Leonard saw it about the same time.

A horse.

A man riding bareback.

One of the men had bridled a horse and was trying to chase us down.

"Fuckin' Lone Ranger," Leonard said.

The Lone Ranger was unsteady on the horse, but he was firing at us with a handgun. A bullet whizzed between us, just missed Herman's back and webbed the windshield.

I reached in the front seat and picked up Herman's Winchester, cocked it, aimed and shot. The horse went down and rolled over, throwing the man. The man stumbled to his feet. The horse didn't move.

"You missed," Brett said.

"No, he didn't," Leonard said. The jeep left the man far behind us, a little fleshy dot against the great landscape of the desert. "Shit, Hap, what did that horse ever do to you? I can't believe you spared that fucker's life and shot the horse. You are some kind of work, brother."

I dropped the Winchester and lay back against the side of the jeep, my head tilted upward. I held my bleeding shoulder and watched the stars bound and bob to the jerks and surges of the ride. Dust came up from the desert and lashed about us and filled my nose. I thought I could still smell blood and gunpowder. The roar of gunfire was in my ears. My legs were starting to shake. I felt as if I might suddenly burst out crying. My ass hurt. I reached around and pulled out the Winchester shells and the revolver that were riding in my back pocket, dropped them on the floor of the jeep. I lay back again and felt weak, so goddamn weak.

Leonard took off his jacket, then his shirt. He gave the shirt to Tillie, who just looked at it. Brett took it and slipped Tillie into it, buttoned it as if she were dressing a small child. It was large enough to make Tillie a short dress.

"Are we going somewhere?" Tillie said.

Brett patted her. The jeep bounced us painfully over rough terrain. I was growing colder. Leonard moved over next to me and turned his coat over and tore out the lining on one side. He stuffed the lining under my shirt, into the shoulder wound. He tied his belt around my leg and pulled it tight by winding the barrel of my revolver in it. He slipped his coat over me, sat with his arm around my shoulders.

"You gonna be all right, Hap," he said.

"Rumble tumble," I said, remembering what Red had called a bad fight. "Rumble tumble."

26

We came to a little road that seemed oddly placed out in the middle of the desert. We drove down the road a ways and came to a little town that looked to be out of an old Western movie. It was at least sixty or seventy years back in time. There were very few lights and there was only one place open, a cantina.

"You sure this is it?" Brett asked.

"Yeah," Herman said. "The airstrip is on the other side of town. It's used for smuggling. Lot of drugs are run from here. The town isn't much, but it's what's out here and it's reasonably close to the border."

Herman drove over to the cantina and parked.

"What are you doin'?" Leonard asked.

"I know Bill and Red," Herman said. "They're more likely to be here than sitting out at the airplane. I got a feeling Irvin isn't far different. They aren't here, it's a short trip to where the plane's supposed to be."

"Make it quick," Leonard said.

Herman went inside. Leonard adjusted the belt on my leg. "Guess it wasn't a major artery," he said. "Stopped bleeding for the most part. I think we can take this off."

"Yeah," I said. "All the blood's on the floor of the jeep."

"How you feelin'?"

"Not good," I said. "I had some moments there where I drifted off. Didn't think I was coming back."

"I knew you were comin' back," Leonard said. "You still gotta get all your shit out of my house."

I turned my head and looked at Brett. The movement was incredibly draining. "Brett?"

She had her arm around Tillie, who had fallen asleep. Tillie had her thumb stuck in her mouth like a baby.

"I'm all right, hon," Brett said. "I'm never gonna forget what you two done for me. Never."

"Ain't over yet," Leonard said. "Hand me that shotgun, just in case there's someone in there got a different plan than the one we made."

Brett handed him the gun. Leonard reached in the coat draped over me, took out a box of shells, carefully loaded the shotgun.

"One thing is," Leonard said, "we can't sit around here. Them people gonna know where we're goin'. Ain't no other place to go south other than this. We put a dent in them 'cause we had surprise on our side and they were fucked up. But when they get straight, ain't gonna be so easy. 'Specially Hap here havin' holes in him."

"Can't believe these shits are hanging out in a saloon," Brett said.

"Irvin and Bill didn't think we'd be coming back, that's why they wanted far away as they could get," Leonard said. "Red, he didn't give a shit. I don't know he cares all that much about Herman, even. I think his mouth could say all kinds of things he doesn't mean. I may kill all of 'em on general principles."

"Been enough killing," I said. "I don't want no more of it."

"You don't always get to choose, Hap."

Herman came out. He had Bill with him. Herman leaned on the jeep, said, "You won't be flying out tonight. Irvin is so stoned he's passed out on the floor next to a jukebox. He got in some kind of fight with a Mexican and got his block knocked off pretty good too."

"Shit," Leonard said.

"What about Red?" Brett asked.

"He's pretty drunk himself," Bill said.

"I was just hoping he was dead," Brett said.

"Hap needs a doctor," Leonard said. "Got any ideas?"

"I can ask around," Bill said. "I think I can find enough Spanish in my memory to do that."

"You do that," Leonard said. "And that doesn't mean drink more first. I want Hap with a doctor. I want him with one pronto. I don't hear from you quick, you're gonna need a doctor. Comprende, amigo?"

"I don't like to be threatened, black man," Bill said.

"It ain't no threat, red man, it's a promise."

Herman got in behind the wheel, started up the Jeep. "We'll be out at the plane," he said.

I passed out somewhere between the little town and the plane, and when I awoke I was lying across the plane's seats, stripped down to my underwear. A little Mexican man with a wart on his cheek about the size of a doorknob and a hairdo that looked to be about three-fourths Wesson oil was poking at me with a pair of long bloody tweezers. There was blood all over the tweezers. He was dropping pellets from my side into a coffee can.

When he saw I was awake, he nodded, smiled, poked the tweezers into my side, pulled out another pellet.

He carefully rolled me on my back and started probing at my shoulder and thigh wound with his fingertips, which didn't look all that clean.

"You have to do that?" I said.

"He doesn't speak English," Herman said.

I turned my head. Sitting nearby were Leonard, Brett, and Herman. Bill was standing up, smoking a cigarette. I didn't see Tillie, Red, or Irvin.

The Mexican turned and spoke to Herman. Herman nodded, said to me, "He says you're not too messed up. Lead went through your shoulder. There's a piece in your thigh that'll take more work than he's willing to do. He's stuffed some gauze in the wound, and he's picked out all the buckshot you got in your side. None of it went in straight on. Just the pellets from the shotgun, and you caught the far edge of the spray. Still, you need blood."

"Then let's get him some blood," Leonard said.

"This guy, he does abortions mostly," Herman said. "Delivers babies. He's not a real doctor."

"Me and Hap had a veterinarian work on us once," Leonard said. "We're not proud."

"He doesn't have access to blood," Herman said. "He's just telling you so you'll know."

"Shit," Leonard said. "I could have told him that."

"What we got to do is sober Irvin up," Brett said.

Bill shook his head. "I don't think so. We're not talking a little drunk, we're talking about being so fuckin' drunk he'll wake up speaking in tongues. Thing we got to do is let him sleep it off, lay around tomorrow, fly out when it's solid dark. Then, if the Border Patrol doesn't catch us, and my guess is they won't because they never have, we end up back at the hangar. You folks go your way, and I go mine, and we never do business again."

"But we can send you a Christmas card?" I said.

"A little candy on Valentine's would be all right too," Bill said.

"All this sounds like a lot of waiting for blood," Leonard said.

"I can make it," I said. "Leonard's just scared I'm going to die and leave my dirty underwear under his couch. Where is Irvin?"

"He's outside under the plane," Bill said. "Me and Herman went and got him. He was still passed out, so we stretched him out there."

"And Red?"

"He was at the cantina, pretty drunk. Doing handstands and stuff. He was trying to make the Mexican drunks in there understand he wanted a big dog to ride and he was showing them his dick, dipping it into a glass of tequila. He passed out on the way here. We left him in the jeep."

"This sitting around bothers me," Leonard said. "Those assholes will change tires on the other jeep, and someone in town will talk."

"They might change tires," Herman said, "but they're going to have hell going anywhere with all the dirt I put in the gas tank. Pissed in it too. And it won't do them a lot of good with the wires ripped out from under the hood and the gear shift bent."

"Good for you, Herman," I said.

"They could come by horse or mule," Leonard said.

"They could," Herman said. "I think they're so stoned they'll do good to stand up, let alone saddle and ride a horse. My guess is they got to wait about as long as Irvin's got to wait."

"From your mouth to God's ear," Brett said.

"Where's Tillie?" I asked.

"At the back of the plane, sleeping," Brett said. "They had her on something strong. Or she had herself on it. She's really wiped out."

"I think we take turns at watch," Leonard said. "I don't like being surprised."

"Very well," Bill said. "I'll go first."

The Mexican held out his hand, said something to Herman. Herman said, "He wants money."

Brett picked up her purse, opened it, gave him a ten dollar bill. "That's pretty close to tapping me out," she said.

"Gracias," said the little Mexican, then fired off something very fast in Spanish, got up, and left.

"What did he say?" I asked.

"He hopes you don't die," Herman said.

It was late at night when I awoke, hurting like holy hell. Brett was sitting on the floor with her head next to the seat where I lay. When I turned to look at her, I saw she was awake.

"How you feeling?" she said.

"Shitty."

"I've got some aspirin. I can get you some water."

"I'd appreciate that."

Brett disappeared for a moment, came back with aspirin and a canteen. She had to hold my head up. I took ten aspirin and a sip of water.

"I owe you, Hap Collins," Brett said.

"Hope you don't think so," I said. "Except in sexual favors, of course."

"I'd give you a blow job, but frankly my guess is your dick stinks and you've bled all over it from your thigh. On top of that, you haven't had a bath in a while."

"Neither have you," I said.

"Yes, but I brought perfume and I never soil my underwear."

"Not even when I make you hot?"

"I guess that's an exception."

"How's Tillie?"

"She's still out. I think she'll be all right, though. It's you I'm worried about."

"I feel weak, but all right. I get something to eat, a big glass of ice tea, and I'll be ready to rock and roll. After a month of bed rest."

"Soon as you get better, what you'll be doing in bed won't pass for rest."

"You're going to have your work cut out for you with Tillie, Brett."

"I know."

"You don't just come out of a life like that and take up choir practice and run supermarket errands."

"I don't know. Maybe Tillie would love that sort of thing now. Maybe she's through rebelling."

"At her age, she's not rebelling, Brett. She's living a lifestyle."

"Don't depress me. Not after all we've accomplished."

"Sorry, baby. I didn't mean to."

27

I slept painfully, but the next morning, just before day-light, I was a little stronger. Out of the pack Bill had brought he produced some tins of sardines. We opened the cans and ate the fish with our fingers. I found that I not only had an appetite, but was feeling better. Not strong enough to jerk my dick, maybe, but at least strong enough to hold it and think about the motions.

After I had eaten, Leonard helped me get into my clothes and shoes. I tried to stand, but couldn't. Leonard went outside and came back carrying Irvin in a fireman's carry. He put Irvin in one of the seats, propped him up and started slapping him.

Not too hard at first, but he picked up the pace.

"Easy," I said.

"You just relax," Leonard said, "and leave the slapping to me."

He slapped Irvin some more. Irvin opened one eye and

tried to grab Leonard's wrist, but Leonard grabbed his, bent Irvin's arm at the elbow, and put a reverse gooseneck on his wrist. It was enough to make Irvin sober for a moment.

"Goddamn!" Irvin said. "You're hurtin' me."

"Man, I hate that," Leonard said. "You done had you a good night's sleep, so what we want for you to do is fly us out of here."

"Fly you out," Irvin said. "I can't even see!"

"What I want," Leonard said, "is for your vision to improve dramatically."

"I'm sick," Irvin said.

"I don't give a shit," Leonard said. "Fly us out."

"In broad daylight!" Irvin said. "You can't do it in broad daylight."

"Is there another place we can park for the day?" Herman asked. "Some place away from this village?"

"I know one or two," Irvin said. "But we're not that well fueled. We'd be stretching it."

"Is it possible?" Leonard asked.

"Yeah, it's possible," Irvin said, "but we might have to fart in the tank to finish out the ride. We make it, it'll be by a cunt hair."

"Where is this place?" Herman asked.

"It's not a landing strip," Irvin said. "It's not even a field like this. It's just a place. I put down there once because I had to. Ground's flat enough, I suppose. It's south of here. But it's stretching the fuel, I'm tellin' you."

"Sittin' here is stretching our odds," Leonard said. Then he called to the back. "Any sardines left?"

"Yeah," Bill said.

"Feed this asshole, and let's go."

"Fuck the sardines," Irvin said. "Don't talk to me about sardines. I can't eat that shit, way I been drinkin'. I don't eat that shit when I'm sober."

"Then you do whatever you need to do short of another drink," Leonard said. "Lift us out of here. Go where you need to go. And come dark, you fly our asses back to Texas. Herman, you want that midget, I'd load him on board now, and get all his little cowboy suit accessories too. And let's keep things like they been. Meanin' people got guns keep guns, and those don't got guns don't get guns. And Herman, I don't much like the fact you got a gun."

Herman didn't respond. He was still carrying the Winchester we had given him. He put it down on the seat next to Leonard, went outside to get Red out of the jeep.

We flew to the spot Irvin had told us about. It was a short and scary flight. Bolts in the plane rattled and we jerked about a lot in the wind. When we landed the day turned very hot and by afternoon I was covered in sweat and sick to my stomach and could only sip water. Inside the plane was like being inside a heated pottery kiln, but I was too weak to go outside, and Leonard assured me it was worse out there.

Red had come out of his drunk talkative as ever. He spent a lot of time complaining about how he felt and what we had done to him and how we had messed up his plans.

Tillie hadn't moved, and if it weren't for Brett checking on her from time to time, I would have thought she was dead.

I propped myself up in the seat, and Brett sat down beside me. "She's really out," she said. "I think I get her home, I got to start her with rehab. I just hope to hell I got money to do rehab."

"Just keep your spirits up," I said.

"Honey, my spirits are so far down they got to look up to see my socks. And then they need binoculars."

*   *   *

As nightfall came I began to get a chill. Leonard put his coat on me again, and Brett sat close, holding me. When it was dark enough, Leonard gave Irvin a little encouragement. "Let's go, shitwipe."

"Leonard missed his calling," Brett said. "He should have been in the diplomatic corps."

"Yeah," I said. "He's got a way with words."

Irvin groaned, got up, and wandered into the open cabin. He sat down behind the controls. Leonard sat in the navigator's seat. Irvin said back to us, "Remember, we don't make it, it's 'cause this bully made me fly without enough fuel."

"We don't make it," Brett said, "it's because your ass was drunk last night when we should have flown out."

Irvin threw up his hands, shifted in his seat to face the controls. "All right," he said. "Contact."

The plane clanked across the rough ground, and when it lifted off it went up fast and at an angle so sharp I thought we were on our way to the moon. The windshield clattered like cold teeth rattling. The engines sounded like a chef chopping cucumbers into slices. The sides of the plane warped and waved.

The air had turned cooler, and up there it was cooler yet. I got the impression the wind was coming in through places that hadn't been there when we left. As we climbed up, so did my sardines, but I fought them down just below my jawline, and when we finally leveled, I looked out my little window and saw the great blackness that was space and the fine white spots that were the stars.

"Jesus Christ," I heard Herman say behind us. "Run this fucker smoother!"

"What you think you're in?" Irvin yelled back. "A 747?"

We flew on and I drifted in and out, mostly out, as the jerks and drops of the plane would bring me awake as soon as I dozed off. I felt cold and feverish at the same time. I looked out the window and saw the night earth running along under us, the plane a great shadow against the moonlit ground.

"How are we?" I asked Brett.

"Good," she said. "I'm glad you were asleep. You missed being scared to death by a land rise, or as we say in East Texas, a mountain. We nearly ran into it. Someone, possibly Mexican Border Patrol, took a shot at us too. There's a hole in the floor near the tail and we think the wing took a shot, and maybe one of the engines. You know that stuff I told you about never soiling my underwear. Well, I was wrong."

"Got any more aspirins?"

"Yeah." Brett pulled her pocket purse out of her coat and got out the aspirins and gave them to me. She went away then and came back with the canteen. I took a handful of aspirins and drank some water.

"What about Tillie?" I asked.

"Still out," Brett said. "Had the shot been another three feet forward, she would have taken it. Shit, Hap. Is this going to end?"

I patted her leg and gave her back the canteen. I turned and looked toward the back. Bill and Herman were sitting in one of the long seats together. Red had one of his own, looking out the porthole, biting his nails. Somewhere along the way he'd lost his cowboy hat and his string tie. There was just him and the soiled suit now. I saw Tillie on the floor, still as the dead.

"Reckon if the Mexican Border Patrol took a shot at us a ways back, we're in Texas now," I said.

Irvin, having overheard us, called from up front. "Actually, we're about to enter Texas. There's a kind of gap in surveillance here, and if we fly low enough, we're okay on radar."

"So how much further to the landing strip?" Red called.

"Not much," Irvin said. "We'll be passing into Texas pretty soon, then we got to do a half circle away from where the law is thick, come into the airstrip low enough to pick vegetables, then I got to land this baby without wadding it up. Which, by the way, takes pretty good skill. The landing strip doesn't have any lights, just a handful of reflectors."

The moment Irvin finished his speech there was a sound like someone had fired a shotgun inside the plane. Briefly, I thought that's exactly what had happened. We were tossed up and back down. I banged my head against the side of the plane, slid halfway to the floor, got my hands under me, pushed myself back into the seat, wished to hell there were seat belts.

Brett was on her knees in the aisle.

"Goddamn!" she said. "Goddamn!"

I reached out and got hold of her and pulled her into the seat, feeling my shoulder tear, my injured thigh stretch. Brett and I looked over our shoulders for Tillie. Tillie had somehow gotten turned longways and was sliding down the aisle toward us on her belly. I glanced at Leonard. He was turned around, riding his seat like a horse.

I heard Irvin say, "Oh shit," and out of the corner of my eye I caught something, jerked my head for a better look. There was a flash of red and yellow on the wing and it swelled and turned orange and licked blue flames at its tips. The plane yawed and coughed and sputtered. The port engine was on fire.

28

Either one of the shots Brett said were fired from below had damaged the engine, or it had finally had all the dust, wasp nests, and lack of maintenance it could stand.

The plane pitched and bucked as if in a carnival ride, lost velocity, then suddenly it was as if you were standing on something you thought was solid only to discover it was actually made of quicksand.

We just dropped.

The flames were wild now and in their glow I could see wisps of black smoke and the smoke coiled and curled around the wing and past the glass.

Brett was in the aisle. She had hold of Tillie, was lying across her. I clung to my seat, glanced up, saw Leonard through the open cabin door. His face looked horrible, his eyes wide.

The plane filled with a noise like a pride of lions roaring, and I realized it was the wind and flames. The fire was licking all along the wing now, tapping at the glass, asking us to invite it in. The wing was melting, becoming a tatter that resembled something made out of chicken wire and blazing toilet tissue.

Then the plane went quiet, except for the roar of the flames, the hiss of the wind. We seemed to float, just float. The right side of the plane jumped and there was a whirling noise. We leaned starboard slightly, started moving forward and down, but at a calculated pace.

I don't know much about planes, but it occurred to me that Irvin had cut the engines. Maybe to stop the gas to the port engine. The flames were still there, but they weren't as high as before. The right engine was all that was working now, and Irvin was using that to bring us down.

I looked out the window, saw the ground was way too fucking close. The plane went silent again, the right engine out of play, the propeller whirling to a stop.

"Out of fuel!" Irvin yelled. "Coasting in. Grab your asses."

Smooth and quiet we went, but like a bullet. I looked out the window at the flames on the wing, saw a stand of dark gnarly trees below us. And I mean just below.

Ahead of us was a clearing, a metal hangar. It was the strip we had departed from. I had a moment of hope. I looked at Brett. She was still lying on top of Tillie, who to the best of my knowledge had yet to twitch an eyelash.

I looked through the cabin doorway. Leonard continued to cling to and ride his chair like a horse. I could see the ground through the windshield. Big hard ground. The plane hit and bounced. It went way up, nose pointing at the sky, then it went back down, bounced again, not so high, bounced some more, then we were darting along the runway.

The wheels screamed, bent under us. Next thing I knew

the plane flipped, spun sideways, and skidded up a dust cloud, and finally, after what seemed about two weeks later, stopped upright, leaning.

I wasn't in my seat anymore. I wasn't sure where I was. I discovered I had hit the wall next to the cockpit. My wounds had opened up. They were running freely. Except for a slight pain in my neck, there didn't seem to be any new injuries.

I looked into the cockpit. Leonard was getting off the floor. Somehow, Irvin had maintained his seat. Then I saw how. He had on a seat belt. He sat there with his head bent forward. Red was getting up between two seats and Herman was sitting on the floor holding his head. Bill was lying on the floor, and from the way part of him was wrapped around the stanchions of one of the seats, I knew he wasn't doing well. Brett and Tillie had slid up under a seat, and I went over there and pulled Brett out. She had a banged forehead, a little blood. I sat her down in a bent seat and pulled Tillie out from under there.

Tillie was snoring. I carried her and lay her across the seat so her head was in Brett's lap. The plane was becoming very warm. I looked out a port window. What was left of the wing was blazing and the side of the plane was starting to catch.

I pulled at the exit door, but it was stuck. I kicked at it and it came open. I got hold of Tillie and tried to lift her, but the wounds, the loss of blood, the crash, it had taken everything out of me. I had to sit down on the floor with her.

Leonard appeared. He picked Tillie up and carried her out. Brett got hold of my arm and helped me out of the plane, onto the ground. Herman and Red followed. Leonard went back in. He came out carrying Irvin, who was unconscious. He went back in and brought Bill out.

When he laid Bill on the ground Bill's body moved like mercury flows. The foot on one leg faced the wrong way.

"He's dead," Leonard said.

"No shit," I said. "What about Irvin?"

"Unconscious."

"I want everyone to relax now," Red said. We turned to look at him. His head was bleeding and his suit jacket was almost ripped off. He was holding one of the Winchesters, pointing it at us.

"From here on out," he said, "we do as I say."

Leonard moved incredibly quick. He grabbed the Winchester by the barrel, snatched it away from Red, whirled it around his head and cracked Red a solid one over the ear. Red decided he had to lie down on that one. He held his head with one hand, said, "Oh God, I think something is broken."

"I advise we get away from the plane," Leonard said. "And if anyone else has any ideas about guns or fighting, let's get it over with now."

No one did.

Leonard kicked Irvin a few times. Irvin grunted, opened an eye. "You can lay here, or you can get up," Leonard said. "Personally, I think what's left of your plane could blow."

Leonard picked up Tillie. Brett gave me a boost and helped me walk. My injuries only hurt now when I walked, breathed, or batted my eyelashes.

I looked back. Herman and Red followed, Red holding his head. Irvin rolled to his hands and knees, crawled, finally made his footing and began to stagger after us.

The plane didn't exactly blow. It just burned and gave off a few muffled pops. It lit up the night sky like an oil well fire.

29

We made our way to the big tin hangar. We had parked our car and Bill's truck in there. Irvin finally caught up with us. He had a key to the shed and he unlocked it. When he pulled the bolt back, Leonard put Tillie down, gave me the Winchester, helped Irvin open the huge doors. Leonard picked Tillie up again, and we went inside.

When we were just in the door, the lights came on.

The shed was full of very large men in very nice suits that had dust on them. One of the very large men was Wilber. He was the only one that didn't have on a nice suit. He had on a cheap suit. He was still wearing his neck brace. He looked like a whiplashed Kodiak bear that had just finished shopping a Sears sale.

One of the men wore a charcoal gray suit with a dark gray shirt and gray and blue tie with red highlights on it. His hair was combed down tight and he had the faintest touch of whiskery shadow. He was smoking a cigar, sitting on an old stool that came with the shed. He had a handkerchief draped over the stool and his ass was on that.

It was Big Jim, and his expression was somewhere between amused and amazed. He had his legs crossed just right so as not to ruin the crease. His shoes appeared to be brand-new. He was looking past us, out the open doors at the blazing plane.

All the big men, except Jim, had big guns. They closed in behind us and pointed their big guns and took the Winchester from me. I didn't try to fight. That would have been useless. Red, bleeding slightly from the head wound Leonard had given him, smiled, limped over, and stood by one of the big men. He looked as happy as an erect dick.

We were searched then. The man who searched Brett spent too much time at it. Leonard had been forced to place Tillie on the ground, and the same man went over and pulled up her shirt and looked at her for a moment.

I said, "They call them women."

The big man grinned at me and held the big automatic he was carrying against his leg and tapped it there, as if trying to decide if shooting me would be more fun than beating me to death.

Big Jim got off the stool, walked past us, stood at the open door and watched the plane burn. He said, "We heard it, but I hate to say we missed it. Anyone get killed?"

"One," I said.

"Ah," Big Jim said, "I'd say that's pretty good odds. One out of all of you. 'Course, you look like hell, and surviving that isn't going to do you any good."

"Red told you we'd be here, didn't he?" I said.

"That's right," Big Jim said. "He called us from someplace in Mexico. Some cantina, wasn't it, Red?"

"Yes, sir," Red said, still a happy erection.

Big Jim went back to his stool. He sat down on it and puffed his cigar. He pulled the cigar from his mouth and pointed the red end in Leonard's and my direction. "You know, it took some balls, you guys to come into my whorehouse like that, shoot Moose in the foot, take my midget. Real balls. I respect that. Really. But, it pisses me off too. Red here, he says he wasn't part of it, but you know, I got to wonder."

Red suddenly looked considerably less erect. "I was kidnapped, Big Jim. Really."

Big Jim looked at Wilber. Wilber didn't move a muscle, didn't flick an eyelash. Big Jim pursed his lips and turned his attention back to Red. "Wilber thinks maybe you were in with them."

"What!" Red said. "No way. No way, Big Jim."

"That's Mr. Big Jim to your little red ass," Big Jim said.

"He wasn't in on anything," Herman said.

"Herman," Big Jim said. "Good to see you. Been a long fuckin' time. I think the Bandito Supremes should have blown your brains out a long time ago. I think maybe they're not as tough as they say. Don't know how much longer I'm going to associate with them. Red here called to tell me he was down in Mexico. He didn't expect you folks to return. But just in case, he wanted to tell me all about you so he could weasel his way back up my ass. I see you folks got Tillie back. My presumption is you found The Farm, and they were all ripped to the tits. Am I correct?"

"Correct," Herman said.

"That's no way to run a business. Personally, I don't allow my men to indulge like that. These Bandito Supremes, they been trading on their reps too long."

"I didn't do anything," Red said.

"I wasn't talking to you, Red," Big Jim said. "Way I see it, I got a whole nest of rotten eggs here. I got the stoned whore who wanted out of my business, then didn't finish her punishment at The Farm. I got the guys came into my whorehouse and shot the foot off Moose. Moose!"

The man Leonard had shot limped from the back. His expensive pant leg was cut back and he was wearing a cast on his foot with metal braces.

"See Moose there," Big Jim said. "He's got to wear that . . . what is it, Moose? Six weeks?"

Moose nodded.

"That's a bad thing to do," Big Jim said. "You guys coming in there like that, causing a ruckus, shooting Moose. He had to rip up some good pants. What, two suits, Moose?"

"Two suits," Moose said.

"Antics like that do not encourage business. That wasn't enough, you go down and get my whore from associates of mine who I was letting use her. I don't like that. And you take my dwarf."

"Midget, sir," Red said.

Big Jim glanced at Red, turned back to us. "You took my dwarf. I don't like that. He may not be worth much, he may even be a traitor—"

"No sir, Big Jim," Red said. "No, sir."

Big Jim turned and looked at Red again, said, "Red, I hear your mouth without asking you to say anything, I'll have you killed. Maybe I'll stuff you, put you in my office for a hat rack. Got me?"

"Yes, sir," Red said.

"Now, where was I? Oh yeah, you come and get my gnome. You maybe convinced him to help you out. Could have been working with you all along. I don't like that. Can't let shit like that go. And look what you done? You've implicated others. I got to kill this other guy now. Who are you, anyway?"

"Irvin. I flew the plane. I'm just someone they hired."

"Too bad, Irvin. The whore, she goes back to work. The woman here, maybe she and me could work something out. I think she could pull some change."

"Not likely," Brett said.

"All right," Big Jim said, "then you get popped too. And Herman, I got to kill you, man. You know how it is? Once you start letting people get away with shit, well, it goes wild. Red here, and Wilber. I forgave them. Let them come back, and it's been nothing but dog shit and piss water ever since. In Wilber's case, that's okay. He's a moron. Right, Wilber?"

Wilber's face jumped slightly, but he nodded. "Yes, sir."

"Yeah, a moron. But the leprechaun here, he knew what he was doing and he talked the moron into it. I shouldn't have let the little shit come back, you know. Like midgets are bad luck anyway, and now, I don't know. Maybe Red had something to do with all this, maybe not. Maybe he's just trying to snake back in 'cause things didn't go the way he wanted. Like with the Tulsa whorehouse. I think wiping him out, that's a way for me to correct an old mistake I should have fixed some time ago. Sometimes I'm too big-hearted, you know?"

I glanced at Red. He was trembling inside his ruined cowboy suit. It was the first time I believe I had actually seen him afraid.

"Well," Leonard said. "You gonna do it, or just talk us to death?"

"Ooooh," Big Jim said. "Feisty. You been watching too much TV, my man. You been seeing too many talky niggers. Where I come from a nigger is still a nigger."

"Where you come from, fuckin' your dog and your

mother are legal," Leonard said. "Or having your dog fuck your mother. It's all the same, ain't it?"

"Boy," said Big Jim, "you really want to die, don't you?"

"Beats having you bore me to death," Leonard said.

"Like I was sayin'," Big Jim said, "you and this fella here, you got balls. But, unfortunately for you, they aren't bulletproof."

"I didn't do anything but fly them," Irvin said. "They paid me and I did it. I didn't know what they were going to do."

"Shut up," Big Jim said. "You think it matters? This shed, it's going to look like the St. Valentine's Day Massacre, I get through here. I got more bullets here than all of you got brain cells. What I got here? Eight guys? Lots of guns. All you dipshits got are your asses."

"Excuse me, Big Jim," said one of the men, "but that fire, it might draw someone."

Big Jim nodded. "We're far out, Hector. But you're right. Might as well get this over with. I believe Wilber would like the opportunity to kill . . . what's your name?" Big Jim pointed to me.

"Hap," I said. "Hap Collins."

"He didn't like the way you treated him in a hotel room," Big Jim said. "That right, moron? A hotel room, wasn't it?"

Wilber said, "Yes, sir."

"Yeah, I bet he didn't," I said, "'cause I whipped his ass. And I kicked it at the whorehouse too."

"There you are," Big Jim said. "Wilber didn't like that. Go ahead and shoot him, Wilber."

"I could have taken you, you hadn't had a gun on me," Wilber said, and he pointed his automatic at me.

"You and about ten like you," I said.

Big Jim said, "Whoa! You really think you could take him, Mr. Hap?"

I nodded.

"What about you, Wilber," Big Jim said. "What do you think?"

"I could take him," Wilber said.

"You really want to fight him, don't you, Wilber?" Big Jim said.

"Yeah, I'll fight him," Wilber said. "Right now."

"I guess you would," Leonard said. "Hap's hurt. He wasn't hurt, he'd wipe your honky motherfucker's shit on the wall."

Big Jim looked about at his entourage. He grinned. They grinned. Red couldn't decide if he ought to shit or go blind.

Big Jim settled his gaze on Leonard, said, "You want to take Wilber instead?"

"Yeah," Leonard said. "I've just traveled from here to Mexico, fought it out with a bunch of would-be bad-asses, eaten badly, slept badly, crashed in a plane on my way back, so I ought to be tuckered just enough to make it a little more of a contest for fat boy here."

Wilber steamed.

Big Jim chuckled. "Hey, you're on."

"What for?" Leonard said. "Just to get shot afterward? What's the point?"

"You win, I let you go," Big Jim said.

Leonard shook his head. "You a man of your word, Big Jim?"

"You trying to gamble with me?" Big Jim said.

"You let me and this walking stack of dog shit fight," Leonard said, "and I win, you got to let me and my man go here. You got to let the woman and the whore go too.

Toss in Irvin here 'cause he's stupid. Herman too. The midget, I don't give a shit."

"I give you your life," Big Jim said.

"Not good enough," Leonard said.

Big Jim shook his head. "I'm going to hate myself in the morning. Okay. I give you Hap, the pilot, the woman, and the whore. Take Herman too. Red, I got plans for."

Red studied Big Jim's face, hoping to see some sign that the plans were positive, but the expression he hoped to see just wasn't there.

"What I say," Big Jim said, "is this. You two fight. One can't stand up when it's over is the loser. My man loses, I let everyone but the troll go."

"I'm not going anywhere without Red," Herman said.

Big Jim turned to look at Herman. "Have it your way." Then back to us. "You lose, colored fella, I got to shoot you all. But I'll make it quick. Promise. I got to tell you, gambling, it's my vice. You got me by the short hairs on that. My wife tells me I'll bet on anything and that I'm too good-hearted. She's right."

Leonard said, "Let me speak to my people."

"Snap it up," Big Jim said. "This plane fire, it could cause problems. Another minute, this offer's no good."

Leonard eased over to us, unbuttoned his shirt, tossed it on the ground. He and Brett helped me to stand. Leonard said, "I don't know he'll keep his word or not. It's all we got, though."

"You're bushed," I said.

"It's not like we got a choice," Leonard said. "Right now you couldn't whip a three-year-old in a straitjacket."

"Come on," Big Jim said. "Enough whispering. Do it."

30

They closed the back door and two suits stood there as guards. The others spread out in a circle around us and Big Jim moved his stool back a few paces. Red slid up against the wall, trying to blend his molecules with it so that he might pass through.

Wilber took off his cheap jacket and tossed it over the side of Bill's pickup bed. He unbuttoned his shirt at the neck and rolled up his sleeves. Wilber gestured at me, said to Leonard, "It's not gonna be as much fun hittin' you as him."

"I'll try to make you laugh," Leonard said.

"He's twice Leonard's size," Brett whispered to me.

"If Leonard isn't too tired, it'll be all right," I said.

Wilber had his legs spread wide and his fist clenched. I could tell then he didn't know shit about technique. Probably never had to use any. When you're that big and strong you can get away with lack of technique.

231

Leonard didn't adopt any stance or posture. He just sort of eased toward Wilber. Wilber suddenly kicked out with his right leg, a stiff, but hard and fast kick. Leonard scooped it up with his left arm and lifted and pushed backward. Wilber flopped to the dirt floor, rolled and came up. Leonard slid into a loose stance, bobbed a little like a boxer.

Wilber grinned at him. This was all great fun. He eased in and threw a wild right. Had it hit Leonard, it would probably have knocked his head somewhere just south of Mexico City.

But Leonard went under the punch, stuck a right in Wilber's ribs, whipped a left to the kidney. Wilber took it well, came around with a backhand swipe that brushed the top of Leonard's head. Leonard hit Wilber with a right uppercut, but Wilber hit Leonard with a left, a chopping blow just over the ear. It sent Leonard to the ground. Wilber kicked him then. Hit him in the face, full blast. Leonard rolled with it as much as possible, but it was a good shot and a spray of blood went wide in the dull lights of the hangar.

Leonard lay on his back, his face bleeding. Wilber planted kick after kick in Leonard's side. Finally Leonard rolled into a kick, got hold of Wilber's leg, and pushed him down. They rolled on the concrete for a moment, then Leonard stuck a finger in Wilber's eye, got loose, got up.

Wilber had a hand over his eye. "You sonofabitch," he said.

He came at Leonard with a wild football kick. Leonard scooped the kick up, twisted, rolled Wilber on his stomach. Leonard stepped over Wilber's leg while he held it, pushed his chest against it and went down. There was a cracking sound like you might hear from a china vase just dropped from an aircraft. It was Wilber's knee going out. Wilber screamed, and Leonard, still locking the leg, bent forward and slipped his arm around Wilber's neck, around the brace, slid his hand into the crook of his other arm and locked that behind Wilber's head.

Wilber was strong and the neck brace kept Leonard from cutting into Wilber's throat with a forearm. Wilber got his hands under him, pushed up enough to roll on his back. But it didn't matter. Leonard lost the leg lock somehow and the ruined leg thrashed out to Wilber's side as Leonard rolled on his back and hooked his heels inside Wilber's thighs and kept choking.

Wilber thrashed and clawed at Leonard's arms so hard he drew blood, but Leonard didn't let go. He just lay on his back with his head pressed tight against the base of Wilber's head, and he kept squeezing. You could see the muscles in his forearms and biceps swell. Leonard moved his foot once, just enough to pop Wilber in the testicles, enough to weaken him. But by that time he didn't really need it. Wilber wasn't clawing anymore. His eyes were sticking way out of his skull and his tongue was skating over his lips. A thin trickle of blood was running out of one nostril and there was a bead of it on his bottom lip.

Leonard flexed even more. The brace was past working for Wilber. Leonard had put so much pressure into it, the brace was beginning to bend, making an indentation for Leonard's forearm.

Leonard turned his head slowly and looked at Big Jim on his stool. Big Jim studied the situation for a moment, made a cutting motion with his hand.

Leonard let go of Wilber, rolled out from under him. Wilber lay on the ground heaving, trying to get his breath back.

Leonard stood up and looked at Big Jim.

Big Jim looked around the room, at us, at his men. He put his cold cigar back in his mouth and pawed around in his suit for his lighter. He lit the cigar and puffed.

"How much money you got?" he asked Leonard.

"What?" Leonard said.

"How much money you got, all of you?" Big Jim said.

Leonard and I had some change, Brett had a few dollars, and Irvin had what was left of the money we had given him. Most of it he had pissed out on the ground after it had turned to beer and then pesos at the cantina.

I said, "Bill's body's out there. He might have some money on him."

"No," Big Jim said. "We'll leave him like he is."

Moose clunked over on his braces and cast, took all our money, bundled it up in one hand, and carried it to Big Jim.

"I got to have something for my troubles," Big Jim said. He counted out the money, frowned, put it in his coat pocket. "I don't like to do a deal where I lose completely. I drove all the way down from Oklahoma for this, and now I'm just going to let you go. But this way I make a little money, and I got Red. Which is what I really wanted. And, I guess I got Herman. Herman, you still have your chance too. I give you that. Red stays. You go."

Herman nodded. "I can't go without Red. You still want to gamble, I'll fight anyone for Red's life."

"Nope," Big Jim said. "That didn't work out so good. Once a night is enough. Someone go over there and get Wilber up. Get his coat. Put him in the car. We'll stop in town, get him a soda."

Two of Big Jim's men picked up Wilber's coat, got hold of Wilber. He screamed in agony when he was lifted. As they carried him along, his leg dragged behind like the tail of a dead animal. They opened the front door and helped him outside.

"This whole thing," Big Jim said. "It's soured my stomach. You know, I'm really a pretty nice guy. I like to give breaks. I'm forgiving. But sometimes, well, you got to know when to cut your losses."

Big Jim reached inside his coat and took out an automatic, said, "Hey, dwarf!"

Red looked at him and Big Jim pulled the trigger. Red's head slammed against the tin wall and the wall went scarlet and Red melted to the floor like butter running off the side of a griddle.

Herman bellowed, charged at Big Jim. Big Jim swiveled slightly on his stool and shot Herman in the head. Herman's charge knocked Big Jim off the stool and Herman came down on top of him.

Two bodyguards leaped forward, grabbed Herman, yanked him off of Jim, rolled him on the ground and shot him several times.

Big Jim said, "He's dead, you fools. He was dead when I shot him."

Big Jim got his feet under him, put his automatic back inside his suit coat and began to brush himself off. One of the bodyguards came over and helped him. Big Jim let him. When he was brushed off he took the handkerchief off the stool and used it to wipe his shoes. He gave the handkerchief to one of his men, turned to us.

"I shouldn't have made a deal like that with you guys," he said. "It was stupid. I thought Wilber could take you, colored man. I thought he'd wipe the place up with you."

"Maybe he had an off day," Leonard said.

Big Jim grinned. "No. I don't think so. All right, ya'll get the whore, get your asses out of here. I don't want to see you no more. I hear from you, I see your faces, whatever, all bets are off. Got me?"

We nodded.

Leonard put on his shirt without buttoning it, picked up Tillie and carried her and put her in the back seat of the car. With Brett's assistance I went after them and leaned against the hood.

Irvin walked past us. He said, "I don't want to never see any of you again. Ever."

Outside, the two bodyguards were putting Wilber into the back of a black Cadillac. There was another black Cadillac parked under the tree next to Irvin's truck.

Irvin got in his truck, started it up, and drove away.

Brett sat with Tillie's head in her lap. I used the car to brace myself and got around to the passenger's side. Leonard got behind the wheel. He said, "Shit, no keys."

"There's a spare in a magnetic box," Brett said. "It's stuck up under the dash there, to the left of the steering wheel."

Leonard found it and we drove out of the hangar.

I turned to look back. Flames from the plane were licking up higher than the hangar. The big men in their nice suits were escorting Jim out to the Cadillac under the tree. He got in and they closed the door. A few of the men got in the same car. The others opened up the trunk of the Cadillac where Wilber waited, then went back inside the hangar.

As we eased away, I saw them come out of the hangar carrying something. The sun shone brightly on the red hair of that something. They dumped Red into the trunk and returned to the hangar.

"Drive very fast," I said.

31

The field across the road was frozen and the ice on the dead grass was very pretty in the moonlight. It was mid-December and Leonard and I were sitting on his front porch looking across the road through barbed wire out where forty acres of cleared land lay. It was a hay field, but for some reason none of it had been baled that year. Bad hay maybe. Perhaps the owner died.

We sat on Leonard's front porch in the porch swing and drank hot chocolate. Bob, Leonard's son the armadillo, was curled up on the edge of the porch, staring out at the night, perhaps thinking about gunfire and shattering dillo shells, relatives gone to that great armadillo den in the sky, or perhaps he was seeing the leering face of Haskel. I wondered if it would matter to Bob if he knew I had given an anonymous tip to the FBI about Haskel's location and vocation. Maybe for armadillos, unlike humans, the past was the past, gone away, completely forgotten.

Whatever, Bob had it cushy now. He followed Leonard about and Leonard shared his vanilla cookies with him more frequently than he did me.

I shifted in the porch swing for more comfort. My right thigh still gave me trouble, and my shoulder was a little stiff. I hadn't gone to the doctor for any of it. Not even blood. I had stayed in bed for a couple of weeks eating steaks and drinking some godawful tonic Leonard made me take. I think I got well so I wouldn't have to drink that tonic.

Brett came out to see me from time to time. I had only actually talked to Tillie once since the events, and all she had said was hi.

We read in the papers about the wrecked plane and the one body found. Bill's. The papers called it a real-life mystery. We had no idea what Big Jim had done with Herman's and Red's corpses, but my guess was they were feeding a mesquite bush in the desert somewhere. Bill's death was attributed to bad flying, and someone believed, or wanted to believe, he had crawled free of the wreckage and died.

Of course, Bill hadn't had a pilot's license, and it had been Irvin's plane. Or at least the one he was using. No future newspaper articles followed. No policeman came tapping at our door.

I think the truth of the matter was the authorities knew who Bill was, had dealt with him before, and didn't give a shit he was gone, just as long as he was out of their hair.

But Bill hadn't been so bad. I thought about how Bill had called that old man uncle, had given him money, bought him beer and cigarettes. I wondered how Irvin had answered to the old man for Bill's death. Or if he had.

I said, "It's funny way it is. I haven't even seen Brett but a few times since October. We only been to bed once. On my birthday. And it wasn't too good, you want to know. I think I'd rather have had a pair of socks or a billfold."

"Maybe you're taking it too personal."

"The bad pussy?"

"How she's treating you, you moron."

"I don't want to say it, but I got to say it. I feel I sort of did something for her I wouldn't have done for nobody but you. And now she's got Tillie back, I'm like last year's used Kotex."

"Tillie needs a lot of attention," Leonard said.

And she did need attention. She was in drug rehab, but she was back to hooking. This time out of LaBorde's two main hotels when they didn't catch her and run her off. Then she'd go to Tyler for a while to hook up with some of the church crowd there, bang them silly.

"You think she's really going to change?" I asked.

"Nope," Leonard said. "I could have told you that from the start. She wanted out of what she was in, but she's not a new person. It could happen I guess, but I wouldn't tie a rubber band around my dick till it did. Do that, your whang will fall off."

"You knew from the start it would turn out like this, didn't you?"

"You didn't do what you did for Tillie, Hap, you did it for Brett. This has got nothing to do with Tillie, far as I'm concerned. Brett for that matter. I did it for you."

"I hate I asked. I hate you had to do it."

"I hate it. But it doesn't matter Brett isn't having anything to do with you now."

"I didn't say she wasn't having anything to do with me."

"Whatever. That doesn't change things. I did it for you and you did it for her because you thought you should do it. We've done it. It's over. What do you want, to be cheered? Have a little parade or something?"

"That would be nice," I said.

"Well, you ain't gonna get it."

"I killed people, Leonard."

"You knew that could happen."

"There were a couple of women back there. I didn't mean for them to die."

"I don't know they had much of a life, Hap."

"And that makes it okay?"

"No, but you think them being women makes anything any different? It makes it done. War's hell. You think shit like this is without consequences, man?"

I pushed against the porch with my foot and the swing moved back and forth for a while. I said, "Would you have strangled Wilber if Jim had let you?"

"In a heartbeat. I'm glad I didn't have to, but I certainly would have. I even liked the idea at the time."

"What about Bill?"

"What about him? He took a chance for money and it didn't work out. I didn't make him do it. He wasn't lied to or convinced. He didn't care, long as he made money. He shouldn't have gone along."

"Well, maybe, but the one bothers me is Herman. Red a little. Herman had turned. Really. He risked his neck and he helped us get Tillie back."

"Yeah, he did. But you know what, Hap? I'm an asshole about it. Guy like that, he'd done enough evil in his time, there weren't enough candles for him to light, enough Hail Marys for him to say. He did all right by us, but he wasn't someone I saw as a future poker buddy anyway. As for Red, he could talk up a good steak ranchero, but he should have died at birth."

"How do you sleep at night, Leonard?"

"I sleep like always. Good. I don't even have Nam flash-backs. I went to do a job I believed in, and I did it. You didn't believe in it, you didn't go. Do you have nightmares about not going?"

"Of course not."

"You would have, had you not done the thing you believed in. It wouldn't have been the same kind of nightmares, but it would have been something. If not a dream, something hollow. That's the way I'd have felt had I let you do that business without me. So, far as I'm concerned, I did what was right. Period."

"And Big Jim gets away scot-free."

"Looks that way. It happens, man. The world don't shake out fair all the time."

"Gets right down to it, I guess it's just you and me, brother."

"Give Brett time."

I nodded.

"I'm going to bed, Hap. Good night."

Leonard stood, gave me a pat on the shoulder, and snapped his fingers at Bob. Bob got up and trotted after him into the house. I'd never seen anything like that. I didn't think armadillos could be domesticated.

"You keep that big armored rat out of the living room," I said. "I don't want him trying to get on the couch with me."

"He thinks it's his couch," Leonard said, and went inside the house.

I sat for a while, nursing chocolate that had gone cold in my cup. The moonlight moved over the field of frozen hay and made it look metallic and sharp. I pulled a deep breath of cold air into my chest and let it out. It felt and tasted like the air that night in the desert some three months, some ten centuries ago.

I thought about the gunfire and the smell of blood and smoke, the strange and horrible passion that had come

241

over me during that time. I think I feared guns and violence because they were so much a part of me. Perhaps no one is more aware of and is enticed by and frightened of violence than the man whose brain is a bomb.

I remembered what Herman had said about the blackness of space, the nothingness between the stars, about the stars being nothing more than dying light.

Bad line of thought, I decided.

I drank the rest of the chocolate, shook out my cup, and went inside.